HOOD CHRONICLES

G.L. GLOWZ

Hood Chronicles
© 2019 by Gloria Sze-Ming O'Koye (G.L. Glowz)

ISBN: 978-1-7380414-4-2

Cover Art by Cre8tive Eye Designs
Illustrations by Sundae Doodles
Edited by Cecilia Ki & Ying Mok

Disclaimer:
This book reflects the author's recollections of
experiences over time. Names, characteristics, events,
and dialogues have been altered to protect identities.
Any similarity to actual persons, living or dead, is
purely coincidental and unintended.

To all my loved ones here and not present

CONTENTS

Backstory of *Hood Chronicles*

The content in this book has been in my heart since I was 15, when I lost a good friend to gun violence. I also wrote this book for my friends that I lost to the streets; I can still hear their voices and their spirits still visit and haunt me in my sleep. I love you all so much, and I have to continuously learn to forgive myself for not being able to see friends who took their last breath alone. I have to put a stop to beating myself up for not being able to change the course of fate, for the lifestyles some were born into, or those who got caught up in the game for the thrill.

Due to the complexity of politics, etc., I kept some of my poetry and stories to myself from a young age because of doubt and fear. Some things that had happened in the past and things that are currently happening will never make sense to me, but I understand that these things may or will continue years after.

To my loved ones who will not see the outside until decades have passed or will never have the chance to taste freedom again, I love and miss you so much. Even though some of you have told me to move on with my life and passion, and to never look back because you feel that you are holding me back... I will not forget... this book is for you all....

You showed me there is more to life, and even in the times my anger almost got the best of me, you made sure you slapped some sense back into my head.... Even those who I hopefully may meet or not in this lifetime.... I have heard your cries from outside those cold walls.... I have taken notice since I was a child, and I want to hear your stories and share them in the future if I have permission to do so.

Just like my other book *A Kintsugi Memoir*, this is another heavy book I have written, but it was also healing to let my writing pull out things I held deep inside my heart. Though there will be pieces I shall take with me when it's my time, I hope the ones that I share will touch my readers' hearts. It's very recently that I decided to finally pour out another area of my soul, and so you have it. *Hood Chronicles*. I ask for my readers to read this with an open heart and open ears, and I would love to expand more in conversations.

Enjoy!!!!

Game Changers

God - To my Creator, The King of kings... You have always sent your guardian angels to protect me, even when I continued to turn my back and choose the wrong paths. There had been times it would have been game over for my life, but You have Your plans for me and I'll follow wherever You want to take me. Even though my trust in You still has a ways to go, I want to rebuild and strengthen the bond. I have faith in Philippians 1:6.

Family - Thank you for being with me, though I have brought grievances to the family due to my carelessness. Also, for encouraging me in the work I do in the community, and a childhood full of knowledge so I wasn't sheltered from the world outside of home. Thank you for clarifications for things I witnessed that didn't make sense to me when I was growing up. To my family that didn't censor anything from me, I love you and thank you.

Fallen Soldiers - I thank you for everything you taught me, for protecting me so I can see another day. Never forgotten.... Memories never faded. I love you... I miss you. We will see each other soon; I will keep pushing forward for us all.

DjChrissay & Willay - My brothers from another mother, we been through Hell and back with our hood adventures (literally). I'm honestly surprised we are all intact (no, seriously, The Lord is good). It has never been a dull moment when it comes to us hanging out. I can never ask for better brothers than the both of you. OddSquad Productions unite!!!!

Nesha - One of my longest friends - we both have gone through so much and you are one of the few people that knows how my heart is. No matter how many times we gave each other the silent treatment, we always pick up where we left off and create new memories. May our friendship continue to mature as we age together.

Tae - You are an amazing friend and always will be, we have too many stories together and even though it has been some time without being in contact with you, if you ever get the chance to read this, just know that I love you and got your back always. You been there and witnessed the things I probably would take to the grave.

To the Neighbourhood Aunties & Uncles - The joy that I am able to call you Granny, Pops, Mommy, etc. there are too many to name, but I want to cherish and thank each and every one of you in my time of need and I'll always remember you in my time of abundance. I'll never forget those who were there for me, listening to me with no judgments and who took me in as if I were your own. From each neighbourhood I was residing and visiting, the love made me feel that I never left the comfort of my home. Thank for the heart-to-heart conversations when I was in my lows and refusing to allow me to completely isolate myself. You provided me shelter, fed me, and taught me about life, and to live instead of just survive.

Nathan Baya - To the one person that I always looked up to for years now, I am honoured to be your friend and continue to watch you grow as an inspiring multi-talented artist. Nathan, I don't think I can tell you how much you have helped me by being yourself. Your authenticity, vulnerability, resilience through your art has always encouraged me. Your events and speeches are powerful, and don't you ever forget that. Don't ever doubt yourself, and I know you will reach for the heavens because your words shall be heard from all four corners of the earth.

CEE Centre of Young Black Professionals - I want to thank each and every one of the staff for replenishing hope in academics, highlighting the potential we have amongst each other and having those with lived experiences being so open. Thank you for going in depth with the Trauma trainings and much needed discussions during the retreat. Thank you all so much.

ShadoozyMusic - I thank you, I thank you and I thank you. Thank you for mentoring me, believing in me even when I wasn't believing in myself in the way I should have been. Thank you for being you.

One Mic Educators - Thank you for amazing opportunities to run workshops in different neighbourhoods, and also for knocking some sense into me when I doubted my art. Thank you for supporting my projects in any way you can. I cherish you and your support is much appreciated.

The Hope Program - Thank you for taking me on as a placement student in the program and teaching me about the ins and outs of the justice system. It has been a humbling experience. Thank you for equipping me with the essential tools so I can be of better service to the population I've loved and been passionate about throughout my life. Your heart is big and I want to thank you for all the work that you do for the youth and families.

Sundae Doodles - You are like totally awesome and I love you so much. Thank you for supporting me on this journey, when we all hang out and work on this project together and your amazing illustrations that capture my messages.

Ying Mok - My sister in Christ, you are one of the realest people I have ever met. We are so much alike that I sometimes sit back and put on a huge smile at this blessing God had put in my life. You are the first I opened up fully to about things in my past and thank you for just listening. I do take full ownership that my sharing can be overwhelming, and I'm grateful that you still chose to be my friend after all this time. I can never ask for a better sister. Thank you for going through my pieces and editing them to the best of your ability.

B.I.U & CMA Entertainment - My Day 1 supporters, I appreciate all of you for believing in my craft and giving me input as I got nervous writing my thoughts in this book. Thank you for listening and giving me the extra push to complete my project. I am forever grateful for having all of you be in my life for more than a decade now.

In Memory of Drew and JV - Though you are not present with us anymore, the community will never forget the legacy that you both had accomplished during your short time with us. The amount of blessings that both of you poured into the communities will never be forgotten. Definition of Game Changers and may both of you sleep in peace.

Hood Chronicles Song List - Part I

Spin El Poeta Feat. Shessi Sandu - Dreams Come True
Boosie Badazz Feat. Shellz - What I Learned From The
  Streetz
Plies - 100 Years
Heartless G. - R1der Mamis
Ace Hood Feat. Plies - Stressin
Gangis Khan - Younger Heads
GizzleStarrMade - Make It Out
Dynesti Williams - Dun The Place
Nix The Truth- Black Image
Plies - Ain't Coming Home
GizzleStarrMade x Golde London - Trapaholic
Carleton - Some Day
Mad Linqz - Black Lives Matter
JB Feat The Game - Fire In Your Eyes
Nix The Truth - Hustlers Stress
Mugsz - Rep Your City
D-Brown Feat. K.A.S.H - Ride For Me
Tupac - Life Goes On
Biggie Smalls - Nobody (Till Somebody Kills You)
J Jon - Statistics
Boosie Badazz - Motherless Child
Ace Hood - Hustlers Prayer
Lola Bunz - Sick
Blacus Ninjah - Hustle On
Webbie - Loving You Is Wrong
Pharah K - Confessions
Boosie Badazz - Dirty World
Blacus Ninjah - Code Round Here
Tupac - Can You Get Away
The Dying Thief - Black Man
Sedrik - Apply Pressure
Golde London - Hip Hop
Reggae Keyz Feat. Mad Linqz - What You Do To Me

Tupac Feat. Jadakiss - Loyal To The Game
EIGHTY - Kingston Nightmares
The Game Ft. Nate Dogg - Where I'm From
50 Cent - Baltimore Love Thing
DT The Artist Feat. Scisk - On Smash
Csin Feat. Glowz - Never Gonna Be The Same
Kanye West - Jesus Walks
Faith Evans -Again
Boosie Badazz Feat. Keyshia Cole x J Cole - Black Heaven
Just Brittany Feat. Zro - Mama Should've Told Me
TnT - Missing You
Coco Leah - What Dreams Are Made Of
The Game - Dreams
Webbie - Momma
Coco Leah - Sunrise
Boosie Badazz - Life That I Dream Of
Boosie Badazz - Waiting For A Visit
T-Rell Feat. Boosie Badazz - My Dawg (remix)
Ojez - Ghetto Gospel
Blood Raw Feat. Lyfe Jennings - Coming Back Home
Queen Ifrica - Serve & Protect
Webbi e-Pops I Love You
Phoenix Pagliacci - Youth Of The Future
Golde London - Juice
DMX - A 'Yo Kato
Plies - Crying In The Shower
Nathan Baya - Pressure
Nathan Baya Feat. Txnix - Pops
Papa Corleone - Amazing Grace
Jah Vinci - In My Life
The Game Ft. Faith Evans - Don't Need Your Love
Keon Love - Relax
Ice Cube - It Was A Good Day
Blacus Ninjah - Skeletor
Gangis Khan - Prayers
Heartless G. - Hills Of Snow

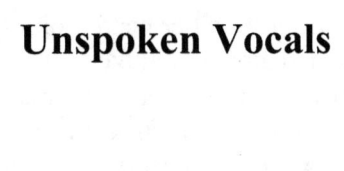

Unspoken Vocals

Junkyard

"Can you take out the trash?"

"Of course, Daddy," 8-year-old Chiamaka replied to her father.

She carefully sorted out the garbage bags to make sure everything was in their rightful place. She picked up two big black bags and carried them out of the suite. She walked to the end of the hallway and turned right to enter the garbage chute area.

Opening the door with her head looking down, she noticed a scent she had not recognized. It wasn't pleasant. She noticed at the corner of her eyes, black figures scurrying away. Something in her gut sent out painful jabs as red flags. Yet she proceeded inside, and silence took over once she raised her head up slowly, as the contents of the bags spilled on the floor. It was a haunting scene that would make her regret stepping inside for the remainder of her life.

Chiamaka's inner child wanted to scream on top of her lungs, yet her hands instinctively covered her mouth as her teeth sink in so deep, the skin's surface broke. She tried to suck out any blood in fear that it would catch up to her in the future. Her chest cried in agony as she tried to remain silent as an eerie presence sent goosebumps throughout her body. She spun around and used her long sleeves to cover her hand to open the knob. She peeked her head out to look both sides to see if anyone was around. She speed-walked back into her suite and ran straight into the washroom. Locking the door and slamming the toilet seat, she fell onto her knees and started to puke profusely.

"Chiamaka, are you alright my child?" Her father asked in a concerned voice.

"Yes, Father," Chiamaka managed to get those words out eventually.

When she was done getting rid of her stomach contents, Chiamaka got up to wash her face before leaning against the wall. Covering her whole face, everything she witnessed started to hit her hard. Crying non-stop without making a sound, she slid onto the floor. A mixture of confusion, sadness and anger swirled inside her mind like a spiral galaxy. Then it happened…. Fear… it crept inside while she was trying to recollect her thoughts. Any reassurance was sucked dry by this dark blackhole and released a Great Depression throughout Chiamaka's body. Yet she would remain silent and move on with her life. Take everything she saw to her grave. Never will anyone truly see what she had witnessed on that fateful day.

Diablo & Ashewo

Was she a distorted guardian angel who wanted to protect? Or was she just another pawn from the devil, striking fear to make a living out of other lives...

"Fuck, what's taking her so long," Kassandra mumbled underneath her breath, pacing back and forth on the sidewalk. She glared at the notorious Scarborough motel across the street. It was five past midnight and the distant screams of addicts struck nerves throughout her body. Just being on this infamous east end road tainted her imagination with morbid depictions.

"I'm going in." She was determined to get her friend out. As she checked her inside pockets, her fingers brushed across an object of significance to her, and a crooked smile spread across her cheeks.

"Hold on, K," Aisha, who was reading from her pager, got up from the public bench to grab Kassandra's hand.

"Angel didn't give us a signal at all." Aisha tightened her grip as Kassandra tried to gently twist her hand free.

"Well, have you ever thought, oh I don't know... SHE WASN'T ABLE TO!!" Kassandra bellowed as she started to lose her patience. Aisha was the logical, give-some-time-before-reacting, calm aura around her. Aisha would be that one person that could fall asleep during an earthquake with a magnitude of 10, and later wake up to an obliterated country asking what happened. She appreciated Aisha's peaceful personality, as she doesn't act out on emotions, which had occasionally saved them from unnecessary drama. But this time, however, could be life or death, which was overwhelming Kassandra inside and out.

"Give it two minutes, you can pop off," Aisha promised Kassandra, as she can sense the demonic fire that's fighting to be unleashed. *Hurry up Angel, I can't control Ms. Apocalypse over here*, Aisha prayed.

Kassandra was the definition of a true ride or die chick, too loyal for her own good. For someone who'd been set up and had a past full of betrayals, she would give you the benefit of the doubt and ride for you to the fullest extent with no regrets. For those who don't put an effort in getting to know her, she could be rough around the edges; the silent one with a screwface that could make a priest agitated. Wearing oversized black hoodies or jackets with multiple pockets and hidden ones that were man-made, no one had ever seen her wear a dress or even shorts since elementary school, other than her family or special occasions in her personal life. She kept it to herself, even when being bullied throughout middle school until now in high school.

Aisha and Kassandra first clicked during the time when Aisha was being harassed by a group of boys, and Kassandra placed herself between Aisha and them. Aisha had been telling them off, when one of the boys smacked her ass and she slapped him. The group surrounded her and taunted her, and Kassandra heard the commotion from the other end of the school hallway. She ran towards them and pulled Aisha behind her while gripping a homemade shank. The boys laughed until Kassandra sliced one of the boy's faces and it infuriated the crew. Aisha thought they were done for, until Kassandra flashed something that was by her waistline. Aisha didn't see what Kassandra was trying to show, but the boys got the message and apologized and scattered.

"Are you strapped?" Aisha whispered, cautious with their surroundings since they say that the walls can hear too.

Kassandra turned around and looked amused.

"No, no, I don't play with those kinds of toys. You alright, ma? Bunch of idiots I tell you," she chuckled.

"Yeah, thank you much, hun!" Aisha replied. She would have dealt with them one way or the other, but it was nice to have another woman stand up for once. She would have easily been "saved" by some guy who wouldn't stand for a "female in distress" but the guys always acted like she owed them a favour. It was from that day on that they became inseparable, even when Aisha got kicked out of school a few weeks after that incident.

"Ya'll miss me bitches!" A loud familiar voice said from across the streets. Aisha gave thanks to the Lord underneath her breath, while Kassandra, not moving an inch of her muscle, glared at the person. It was Angel, cheerfully doing her victory march as a signal that it was a successful night. Angel gave Aisha a big hug and turned around, startled by Kassandra's death stare.

"Ah wah kind of screwface yuh wear pon your face? Girllll, you better straighten that shit up before you really become the Grinch!" Angel exclaimed. Kassandra held her stance, which made Angel sigh and she gave Kassandra a big hug.

"Okay, okay, okay, I'm sorry that it took a bit longer than expected, but him and his friends wanted more services that I couldn't resist offering a package deal," Angel explained. Deep down, Angel hoped that Kassandra would be pleased with the extra earnings, since it would mean more profit from her cut. She reached into her Coach handbag and pulled up a stack of 50s and 20s, which she counted it and gave a portion to Kassandra.

"Here's extra for causing you distress." Angel put in a few more 50-dollar bills, along with her puppy face. Kassandra shook her head and rolled the money up to put in one of her pockets.

"Let's get out of here," Kassandra said with a stern voice, as she had both Angel and Aisha walk ahead of her.

Kassandra got home and looked at the clock and saw it was around four in the morning. She took off her jacket, took the cash out, and placed it in her hidden stash in her room. When she checked the other rooms, she found her grandma and mom sleeping. She went to the kitchen and opened the cupboards and fridge – she could use some of her earnings to buy some groceries on the weekend. She went to start the stove and put a pot of water to boil, so she could have some wontons to eat before heading to bed. Kassandra then went to the bathroom, peeled off her clothes, and got into the shower. Rinsing her body to wash away the energy from the outside down the drain, she reminisced about how it all began....

Kassandra's story began when her father had become absent once more, after spending five years with her family, in the Halloween of grade 9. Two months after his departure, while walking back home through a small forest by her school, she was raped by a familiar face in her neighbourhood. Three days after the incident, a rumour of Kassandra being sexually active spread like an epidemic; she never told anyone of her rape since she wanted to take that to the grave. *They don't like me anyways, if they want to believe it, then so be it. I'm not going to waste my breath,* Kassandra told herself. She valued her virginity, and she felt worthless, so she started to isolate herself. Isolation and depression were making her vulnerable and a prime target for recruiters to try to get her into the sex trade – or so they thought. Little did they realize that these setbacks only fed into her fighting spirit.

A girl named Bianca, who was a year older than Kassandra, had befriended her after the rumour had spread. Bianca was one of the most popular girls in school. She loved to socialize and had no problem knocking out anyone that rubbed her the wrong way. She put on quite a lot of makeup and would come to school with some of the freshest outfits. She was up to date in fashion and would set trends in the school.

Kassandra just assumed Bianca came from a rich family and never questioned where the money came from. Bianca would buy both of them big meals and would give cash to her in an attempt to try to get her to dress up. That would never work; Kassandra only got more men's clothing and filled up her toolkit. She later understood that Bianca was trying to condition her. The two of them hung out every day after school, and they got to build a bond.

Bianca gradually revealed how she had been getting money to support her everlasting appetite for materialism. She shared with Kassandra how she moved to Canada with her aunt from Florida. Bianca had been close to her father until he got incarcerated in another state, and she rarely got to see her mom often since she was still in Jamaica. She wasn't close with her aunt, other than being scolded once in a while; her aunt gave her a lot of independence. Kassandra grew fond of Bianca and saw her as the older sister she had always wanted. Bianca began to take Kassandra to different places and tell her to wait while she made money and would start to introduce new people to her.

"Why you so uptight for?" Bianca would always ask Kassandra when there was male company. Kassandra noticed that Bianca preferred to hang out with older men. Age wasn't the issue for her – it was the fact that they would look at her lustfully and made remarks that showed their intention. Kassandra quickly shot down any advancements, and most guys would back off. But when Bianca showed Kassandra her girl friends, her wall would come down and she had this protective nature for them.

Kassandra snapped out of her meditative zone and got out of the shower. She rushed to wipe herself dry with a towel and put on an extra large ruby red t-shirt with a pair of black boyshorts. She went to comb her wavy black curls before pulling her hair into a sleek ponytail. There were no plans to be in a deep slumber, since school would be in the next few hours; only power naps she would allow herself to take. She went to make her meal, ate it quietly and washed the dishes. She laid by her family couch in the living room and turned on the TV with the volume muted. They were running some animal documentaries, and Kassandra started to reflect on her past till she slowly drifted off to sleep.

One day, Bianca had asked Kassandra to come with her to one of her homeboy's cribs. When they got there, they found themselves sitting in a living room with about five other guys. Bianca then told Kassandra to accompany her upstairs to one of the bedrooms to help her fix her bra.

Something was off about the room when they got inside, and Bianca told her to wait while excusing herself to the washroom. Kassandra could hear mumbling outside the door and couldn't quite make out the words. Suddenly the five guys from the living room rushed inside and turned off the lights. Kassandra screamed out for Bianca and ran to the door trying to open it. *Fuck Fuck Fuck I'm going to die!* Her mind raced as the door wouldn't budge. She tried kicking it right before she felt someone trying to put her into a chokehold and another one trying to grab her legs.

"Stop fighting, bitch, and take this dick!!!" One of the guys yelled before slapping her across her face.

"Drag her to the bed, fucking whore!" Another one shouted across the room.

"Cover her mouth! She's too loud!!" a third voice roared. The voices seemed endless in the ordeal.

Kassandra felt a strong hand gripping her mouth, smothering any sounds she was making. Her pants were getting pulled off, while someone was squeezing her throat, constricting the air flow.

Then it happened….

In the midst of the chaos, Kassandra heard someone coughing up mucus before she felt a wet, sticky substance land on her face near her mouth.

"Stupid bitch, once we done, you a goner!" A familiar voice stopped Kassandra's heart for a brief moment. She didn't remember seeing him when they walked in, but it clicked in that one of the guys was slouching on the couch with his fitted hat covering his eyes. The same one that had ripped her sacred temple not too long ago, the same voice that haunted her every night before she cried herself to sleep.

The fear she had before turned into pure rage. The spirit of Kassandra was slaughtered and from the depths of the abyss in her earthly shell, her newly discovered alter ego was birthed from that very moment.

Diablo was born….

Diablo took over Kassandra's whole being and started to throw blows and landed them on her attackers' bodies. She heard wailing and screaming from different voices in all directions, which only fed her thirst for blood. One of the guys tried to wrap her throat with his muscular arms, but Diablo slammed the both of them to where she saw the table and heard the mirror crashing down, shattering shards, causing more distress to the occupants in the room. She grabbed the first object she could get her hands on and went to work. The struggle continued endlessly till the howling of excruciating pain from her attackers gave Diablo's fury an orgasm.

Bianca was in the other bedroom waiting for the boys to finish with her, before coming inside to check up. Kassandra was gorgeous and with both of them working together, they would be living well off. Plus, her feistiness would be perfect role play for the customers, which Bianca could attempt to charge extra for. She liked Kassandra; Bianca shared secrets of her past to her that she hadn't told anyone at all in her life. In a twisted way, Kassandra was like the little sister she always wanted.

The other girls she was recruiting, she couldn't care less what happened to them. But Kassandra, she wanted to make sure she would give her best clients to, and she could see herself and Kassandra moving in together. *First, she must be initiated in*, Bianca had in mind when setting her up. There was a feeling of guilt creeping into Bianca's mind, but she brushed it off. It would be over, and the person Kassandra is, Bianca could talk her way out of being involved in the situation. But Bianca jumped when she heard the mirror crashing and hesitated to open the door. She ran and budged the door once she heard the screams. She opened the door and puked at the sight.

"Kassandra!" Bianca called for her in a shocked state.

Like a successful exorcism, Diablo disappeared, and Kassandra returned, exhausted from the ordeal. Bianca stopped breathing till she heard all the guys moaning in pain, which brought her relief. She supported Kassandra in getting up and they both left the place to get to Bianca's place. Luckily, her basement had a separate entrance, so they got in with ease. Assessing Kassandra, it looked like she only sustained minor injuries, with tons of bruises.

Bianca got her first aid kit in her bedroom and started to tend to Kassandra's wounds.

"What took you so long, Bianca? I was calling for you and you weren't nowhere to be found." Kassandra voice cracked while trying to seek answers. Her teary eyes couldn't mask the destruction that happened in that room.

Bianca had underestimated Kassandra's strength and her will to fight. *She is more useful keeping track and being the bodyguard*, she decided. She had broken bread with Kassandra already, and giving her a cut should satisfy her and keep her tame. She listened and hugged Kassandra as she went through her emotions throughout the night.

Kassandra didn't want to believe that Bianca would put her in that position, and so she continued to be in denial and remained close to Bianca.

Kassandra woke up to her grandma's cooking, and also the Hello Kitty alarm clock she had set for 8 o'clock. She changed into her large red hoodie and black pants and went to eat some of the congee that was on the stove. She grabbed her black backpack stuffed with books and headed out to school. Bianca was chilling by the corner where Kassandra's math class was, and she signaled for Kassandra to follow her into the washroom. Once Bianca checked the premises to see that people were in their classes, she gave Kassandra an agenda booklet and placed it in her hand.

"It's going to be a busy weekend. Q called me and has his friends from New York coming to spend a week in

Toronto. I called Mystery and Angel so we can put on a show together. We are going to be set for a good few weeks after this," Bianca eyes twinkled. Kassandra went through the notes in the book and made mental notes.

"Imma need you to behave yourself, they're lawyers and one is a judge.... We all gonna eat good," Bianca smiled. *Just like doctors, officers and even pastors*, Kassandra kissed her teeth. Nothing surprised her anymore after the first big clients she witnessed. Bianca had some high-profile clientele at her disposal, and as much as Kassandra resented these johns, she was glad the majority of them had every reason to be discreet, so they were on their best behaviour.

"As long you girls are okay, I'll be polite," Kassandra replied. This was a promise she made as she crossed her fingers behind her back.

It had been months since the incident. Bianca had given some time for Kassandra to heal from the ordeal and was always there whenever she had her mental breakdowns. Bianca started to propose to Kassandra about the job she wanted her to do, yet Kassandra was resistant to the new idea, not wanting to be retraumatized.

"I need protection, Kassandra," Bianca urged. "Plus, it's a nice income." Money may be tight at times, but it wasn't appealing enough to put her sanity at risk.

However, once Bianca mentioned the fear she would strike in the men's eyes, something sinister bubbled inside of Kassandra. The thought of striking at unexpected men filled her with glee. Thinking of their power-hungry asses trembling and screaming for mercy had her biting her lips in pleasure. Out of all the "benefits" Bianca used to woo her with, Kassandra was won over by the promise of being able to become the predator to the lust-filled predators.

Bianca taught Kassandra about bookkeeping, going through protocols if anything were to happen, and codes they would use to communicate when on the job. Bianca also encouraged Kassandra to get girls in the clique, where they would pay Bianca for hooking them up with the clientele and Kassandra for protecting them.

Kassandra felt it was wrong to lure innocent girls, but when she started to see the signs of girls being pimped by men and being ripped off of their earnings, she would step in. She couldn't stand how some of the pimps were taking all the profit or taking 60 percent while giving the girls 40. Some of the girls were so used to being ripped off, they would keep offering Kassandra money, while she was just glad they got out of their previous situations. Yet they were eager to pay her, so eventually she caved in and asked for a maximum of 15 percent and nothing more.

Through her work, she met a lot of women, some she can bet that society wouldn't even think would be involved. Kassandra had to decline some of the romantic advances from some of the women, since she refused to mix business with pleasure, and deep down, she felt that it would be taking advantage of the women.

She particularly grew fond of Angel, whom she met one night by a spa out of town. Bianca had a girl who Kassandra was to look after, and she was working in a spa hidden from the public eye. Kassandra kept missing the place, because it was located in what looked like a business building. When she walked in, the place looked like a gentlemen's club. There was a medium-sized pond with a dragon fountain, lotus flowers and lily pads in the pond with different sized koi fish swimming around. String, piano and flute music played in the background, and large posters of different girls were displayed on each side of a narrow hallway leading to the back. She was greeted by a receptionist who looked at her and interrogated her. *Probably thinks I'm an undercover*, Kassandra thought. The receptionist grew less tense when a girl of Oriental descent went to hug Kassandra.

"Diablo!!! B told me so much about you! I go by Angel." The girl played with her hair, putting on a beautiful bright smile. She was wearing a pink floral lace longline lingerie set, with pink stilettos. Angel was a very beautiful woman inside and out. Kassandra wondered what had her working in this type of industry but knew better than to fuel her own saviour complex. Their introduction was interrupted by a middle-aged Caucasian man, who reeked of the smell of alcohol. He stormed out of one of the rooms from the back and stumbled towards them.

"I'm not done with you yet, stupid Chink," he staggered while sticking his middle finger to Angel.

"Oh, shut the fuck up, Cracker," Angel replied while rolling her eyes, "You only paid for 15 mins of a blowjob, if you want it longer, pay up, broke ass." She slapped one of her hands to the other.

"Glenroy, I am going to have to tell you to get out, I'm calling a cab." The receptionist attempted to diffuse the

30

tension stirring up, not wanting any negative attention that may harm business.

The man stumbled closer with his fist in the air, wanting to hit Angel. Angel put her hands over her face to prepare for blows.

Kassandra grabbed the man's wrists tightly and pinned them to both his sides. "Sir, I need you to calm down, you're intoxicated," she tried to reason with him.

The man looked at Kassandra and burped into her face before shoving her back.

"Stupid nigger, mind your own fucking business." The man started to collect phlegm in his throat, about to aim at her face.

That's when Kassandra lost it as Diablo took over her, and she gave the man a hard-left cut before sending his brain bouncing inside his skull with an uppercut. The receptionist screeched, while Angel smiled as she told her to calm down. Diablo kicked the side of the groaning man before grabbing his underarms and dragging him to the back door. She was about to do real damage to him, now that they were away from prying eyes. She must have been consumed with anger, as she didn't notice that Angel had opened the door with two muscular Oriental men; both had their arms covered with tattoos that she instantly recognized as a Triad clan. Frustrated, Diablo backed down and allowed Kassandra to take over once again, allowing the two men to escort the hostile person away.

"Oooo... Bianca knows how to pick them, I really want to thank you." Angel gave Kassandra a seductive look. *Not again,* Kassandra shook her head, *I need to take a break from this before they try spiking my drink and I wake up with one of them.*

"What's up with him?" Kassandra asked, diverting the conversation.

"Oh Glenroy, he's always grumpy. He's a nice fellow, poor guy's wife left him for a guy close to her age once she got her citizenship. He was talking to another pretty girl from Japan, but I guess they got into an argument or something," Angel answered, shrugging her shoulders.

"He was off today, usually he would go for the diamond package, but today he just went for the a la carte," Angel sighed, disappointed that her regular customer had a blowout. "Thank you again though, Diablo, I would hate to lose my favourite customer."

"You can call me Kassandra," she replied, as she got ready to leave.

"Such a pretty name, I might just give you mine one of these days," Angel winked. Angel gave Kassandra her money and kissed her cheek before they parted ways.

Days passed and the big weekend finally came. Kassandra wore a red tank top with baggy black pants. She put on a black and gold Crooks & Castles jacket with inside pockets she made and put in all her tools for the night. She put on these red, black and white Jordans that Angel had given her as a gift, and put her hair up into a tight bun before putting a gold hairpin in. She folded some money and placed them neatly into the shoes for emergency funds. She waited until the sun set, after her family went into deep sleep, then she crept out and walked a few blocks east to wait for the girls. Aisha bumped into Kassandra at the bus stop, where she planned to meet Bianca, Angel and Mystery, to head down to their destination. Angel's oldest brother, who knew everything about Angel, would be driving them there and back.

"Hey, where are you heading tonight looking so fly?" Aisha looked at the sky before meeting her eyes with Kassandra.

"Handling some business with the girls," Kassandra replied, while checking the roads for anything signs of the vehicle.

"I see…. How much longer will you do this?" Aisha's question threw Kassandra off.

"What are you talking about?" Kassandra demanded for more clarity.

"I mean, this… I'm always here for you and I even came with you on some of the trips you've taken, but I'm scared, Kassandra, I'm scared for you." Aisha's voice was chipping as she fought off her emotions.

Kassandra knew Aisha had an issue with Bianca and always mentioned that Bianca was setting her up but stopped when Kassandra snapped at her. They had stopped talking to one another for some time, until Kassandra went to her house one day and Aisha opened the door crying, embracing each other as they promised to stop allowing others to get in between their friendship. Since then, Aisha had always been there by Kassandra's side; either she accompanied Kassandra on the mission or made sure they talked on the phone when Kassandra came back.

"Nothing is going to happen, Aisha, you know I'll be good." Kassandra pulled out a tissue and wiped Aisha's tears.

"I love you, Kassandra, you're the only one that understands me other than my grandma. I'll lose it if anything happens to you." Aisha was determined to get her message across.

"Aisha, don't do this to me now. We can talk when I come back, I promise." Kassandra was fighting back her emotions. *Why are you doing this now, Aisha?* Her mind started to ponder. She had never seen Aisha being so boldly vulnerable.

"I'm coming with you, Kassandra. Tonight, I'm not taking any chances." Aisha's stern look had Kassandra speechless. Their intimate moment was disrupted by honking from a speeding vehicle from a near distance.

"Girl, you're so lucky my brother took the big whip," Angel said, annoyed that Aisha was joining them.

Angel had wanted Kassandra to be less tense for tonight's big show. Maybe after business the girls can all have fun together. Now with Aisha on Kassandra like a German Shepherd, all of Kassandra's attention would be on her. *They probably fucked*, she thought, as she sneered at Aisha on the rear mirror from the passenger seat.

Aisha gave cold one-word answers to the other occupants in the car, while sharing fruitful talks and heart-filled laughter with Kassandra.

Bianca was also agitated with Aisha, but she kept her feelings to herself. *Whatever, whoever keeps Kassandra in check is in my good books,* she continued to remind herself.

The trip felt like forever as the car went on the highway. Kassandra was grateful that Aisha was with her – she didn't mind the other girls, but Angel had been aggressive in her advancements lately.

Kassandra could recall a few days ago, when she went to Angel's place after a meeting with a client ended badly. She wanted to make sure the john didn't follow their cab home. She was tired, so Angel told her to crash on her couch for a bit. *Just only for an hour,* Kassandra thought.

She told her family she'll be sleeping over at Aisha's place and Aisha followed through with the story. Angel gave her a white tank top and with black booty shorts, and though Kassandra tried to protest, she gave in with little resistance and hopped in the shower. When she was down, she dropped right on the couch and snored. Kassandra later woke up a bit by some movement but ignored it to go back to sleep, closing her eyelids.

Suddenly she felt her shorts being pulled, and a wet kiss placed on her inner thigh. Kassandra got up and pushed a naked Angel off of her. Angel squealed as she fell onto the floor, then started to laugh uncontrollably as Kassandra pulled her shorts up and stood on the couch.

"What the hell were you doing?!" Kassandra shrieked as she jumped off the couch and scurried to put her clothes on.

"I was trying to surprise you, but I guess you're not the one who likes them," Angel replied with a smirk.

"Have you lost your damn mind, woman!" Kassandra couldn't believe she had to put her foot down.

"I should be asking you that. You made it sound like you woke up with a gun to your head!" Angel replied, still laughing at Kassandra's overreaction. Kassandra said her goodbyes and almost tripped trying to run. That would be the last time she would crash in any of the girls' cribs.

"Kassandra, we need you in the room tonight." Bianca gave her a heads up as all the girls got out of the car. They had reached their destination and it was splendid from the outside, an enormous mansion out of nowhere. It was like a castle marking its territory among the vast land, an unknown mystery that held secrets from the world. The car went to park somewhere in close proximity, waiting patiently until it was time to go home.

The girls went to the door, and Bianca grabbed the ring pull and knocked it a few times. They heard footsteps before silence, then the door opened with a man of African descent, around late 40's with an athletic build. He didn't speak and motioned the girls to come in. He led them up a magnificent marble stairway into a big room with a group of four black men in suits before he joined in sitting with them.

Kassandra started to become anxious and began screwing up her face but snapped out of it and put on her poker face. Kassandra and Aisha stayed by the doors, while the other girls went to give the men hugs and kisses on the cheeks. Mystery sat on one of the men and started to make out with them, while Angel let another fondle with her breasts, before putting one of them in his mouth. Bianca was sitting next to one of the men, who seemed to have this aura of an authority figure around him. Kassandra also had a feeling that he would be much trouble if things went sour. The two had a brief discussion before the man handed her a large brown paper bag. Bianca opened it and smiled. She walked up to Kassandra and Aisha and handed Aisha the bag.

"Here's the loot, they gon pay more the more stuff we do," Bianca grinned.

Bianca went to sofas in the room and Kassandra and Aisha followed and sat down.

"You in for a show, bitches," Bianca said as she spun around and walked towards the table. She went to this other room at the far back and came out with a big white blanket and placed it on the floor. Angel and Mystery got up from the men and helped Bianca flatten and smooth out the blanket, and one of the guys brought up bottles to each of the three girls.

"What about those two? Are they part of your clique?" One of the guys pointed in the direction of Kassandra and Aisha.

"No, Dodzi, they just came here to accompany us," Bianca explained, already stripped to her pink laced up bra and G-string.

37

"Such a shame, they look so beautiful, I'll pay good money to eat them out," Dodzi looked at Aisha lustfully.

"She's not involved, buddy," Kassandra hissed as she put her arm in front of Aisha.

"I'm so sorry, didn't know you two swing that way." Dodzi put his hands up and backed away.

Angel and Mystery were fully naked, and Bianca poured sensual oil all over them as they rubbed each other. The men in the room directed all their attention to the three girls as they started to foreplay with one another.

Performing (cunnilingus), the room filled with moans and groans as the sexual tension started to build up. The men continued to approach Kassandra and Aisha and handed them money, before joining in with Mystery and Angel and Bianca. It seemed like forever for Kassandra; she just wanted to get out of the room. Aisha nudged Kassandra to help flatten and count the money. *At least this should help kill time*, she thought as she slowly recounted the cash to make sure they weren't missing even a cent.

Finally, the other girls wrapped up their performances with the men, and the guys went to clean up in another room.

"We going to freshen up, and we gon dip. Can one of you girls call Angel's bro to get ready" Bianca told Kassandra and Aisha. The girls disappeared into a different room, leaving Kassandra and Aisha to clean up the main room. They both patiently waited by the door for the girls with everyone's bags.

"Excuse me, miss," the man who first gave Bianca the deposit spoke to Aisha. He was in a towel and walked towards Kassandra and Aisha.

"How may we help you, sir?" Aisha replied, looking up and down with a disgusted face.

"No need to stink up your face, little girl, I was talking to your friend." The man gave a dirty look to Aisha.

Aisha shot the man back with a glare and kissed her teeth. Kassandra prayed for Aisha to not set off anyone. She was not in the mood for things to go sideways.

"I apologize for my rudeness. I go by Mark. What is your name?" Mark asked Kassandra.

"Her name is Diablo," Aisha answered. "Ouch!! What was that for?" She exclaimed as Kassandra elbowed her.

"Can you behave yourself?" Kassandra gave a stern whisper.

"You really are something else." Mark shook his head at Aisha, while Kassandra held Aisha, who was growling back.

"You two were awfully quiet. Such a shame you both didn't join in. The more the merrier," Mark chuckled.

These girls need to wrap up ASAP, Kassandra's mind was going a mile a minute.

"Go check on the girls, Aisha, let's go," Kassandra told Aisha quietly. Aisha gave a quick nod and went towards the other rooms.

"Yeah, not my type of party. Nice meeting you though, Mark." Kassandra extended her hand for Mark to shake.

Mark went to shake Kassandra's hand but wouldn't let go.

I fucked up, I'm so stupid, Kassandra heart was pacing at her potentially lethal mistake. Why did she allow herself to be so vulnerable?

"Can you kindly let go of my hand, Mark?" Kassandra said assertively, as she tried to twist her hand to loosen from Mark's grip. He only held on tighter, before using his other hand to grab Kassandra's tank top, and a tearing noise could be heard from the stretching.

"Let's have fun baby.... They call you Diablo, let's play a devil's game, shall we?" Mark pulled Kassandra closer, kissing up her neck. She squirmed and tried to maintain her posture. She didn't want to cause a scene.

"Let go of me, Mark." Kassandra started to get angry. She managed to dig her nails into Mark's face, and it dug into his eyebrows before she dragged her nails down to his chin. But he was just too strong and sucked hard on her neck. Kassandra lost her cool, and as soon as Mark let go of her neck, she mustered all the strength she had and headbutted the man with all her might.

"What the fuck is wrong with you!" Mark screamed in pain as he held his head.

"I told you to fucking let go! Shit, your head is as hard as a motherfucker!" Kassandra shouted back, while holding her head. Her brain felt like it was bouncing on a trampoline.

"What the hell is going on?!" Aisha ran out alongside the other girls, with Dodzi and the other three men following close behind.

"This bitch headbutted me!" Mark pointed at Kassandra while still holding his head with his other hand.

"I told this nigga to let me go, and he refused." Kassandra was trying to shake her headache off.

"Don't call me a nigga, I ain't no nigga!" Mark shouted.

"Well you sure are ignorant, and that makes you a nigga, NIGGA!" Kassandra shouted back.

"Cut the crap out, the both of you!" Bianca got in between the two hotheads.

"Don't be disrespecting my friend, stupid whore!" Dodzi stuck his middle finger at Kassandra while the other three men checked on Mark.

"Just because your two little sluts didn't join, doesn't make you any more of a saint!" Dodzi continued to push buttons.

"What are you trying to imply, asshole?" Aisha spoke from the side.

"Shut your mouth, tramp," Dodzi shot back.

Kassandra was starting to fume, and her vision started to become blood red. Bianca could feel Diablo slowly emerging and motioned for Angel to go get her brother. Angel got the message and made her way to the door. But one of the three guys grabbed her wrist.

"Where do you think you're going?" The man pulled Angel towards him and gave her a chokehold.

"Let my girl go!" Mystery shouted and started flaring up, throwing blows at the man's back. The other two subdued her, while Angel used her heel and dug it into the man's foot, which made him loosen his grip.

Aisha started to fight Dodzi by kicking his balls and biting the other three men to free up Mystery.

Bianca watched in horror at the brawl that was unfolding and almost in slow motion, she saw Diablo emerge from Kassandra's cocoon; like a demon-possessed person, she screamed and started attacking the men.

"Kassandra, STOP!" Bianca's cries went unheard.

Angel bolted through the door to grab her brother, while the big struggle ensued. Aisha was kicking Dodzi's head, before he managed to grab her foot. Dodzi pulled Aisha down and started choking her. Diablo snuffed Dodzi with a right and left hook, then proceeded to grab his head back. Diablo wanted to rip his head out, but Bianca managed to intervene. Aisha got up and started stomping on Dodzi, before Bianca managed to grab her and then both of them fell down. Diablo was breathing hard as she started to black out. All she heard were screams from everywhere. She suddenly felt Mark slapping her face and she got see him forming a fist, ready to K.O. her. She was ready to take the blow, but Aisha stood in front and she could hear a loud crack when the fist and Aisha's face made impact. Diablo remembered her partners in crime. She retrieved one of the objects from her inside pockets and became a beast, lost in complete darkness.

Bianca and Mystery were able to pull Aisha away from the commotion, and watched Diablo creating a path of destruction. Diablo left Dodzi and the other men on the floor almost lifeless, but their pride took more damage than their physical form. However, Mark was able to overpower Diablo, and had the scythe of death at her throat.

"You going to die, you stupid bitch, I'll fuck your corpse just for the pleasure of it." Mark had the eyes of a killer.

Diablo did a good amount of damage to Mark's face, and he was about to send Diablo to where her alter ego belonged, in Hell. But Kassandra was still trapped, meaning this would be her ultimate end.

"I advise you to back the fuck off, before I light up this whole motherfucking place." Angel's brother rushed in with Angel behind him.

Mark got up and Angel's brother pushed him down, before giving him a hard stomp on his head, leaving Mark knocked out cold.

"Damn, shawty, you almost met Saint Peter if I came any later." Angel's brother extended his hand to support Diablo getting up.

"Whoa whoa, chill ma… can't get a man who can't bite back." Angel's brother held Diablo as she tried to attack Mark.

"It's done, let it go," Angel pleaded. "We need to take Aisha to the hospital and to get all of us checked out." She finally got Diablo to subside and Kassandra came back.

Angel helped Kassandra get into the car. While she and Aisha rested, the other girls and Angel's brother stayed back a bit to make sure all grounds were covered. They made Mark, Dodzi and the other men vow an oath of silence. Neither party could afford anyone to know what happened in the house, so the situation was placed in the vault of the past, forever.

When they got back, Angel's brother sped back into the city, to the nearest hospital. Fortunately, Aisha's injury wasn't serious enough to leave any permanent damage, and with bed rest and checkups, Aisha was able to make a full recovery.

But that night left everyone traumatized, and the girls took a long break from the business to do other things. After a while, Bianca started to lust for the money and go back into the work. Kassandra, still shook from that night, refused her for a few times, but started to come around, out of her concern for Bianca's safety.

On one summer morning, Kassandra, Angel and Bianca were hanging around on a beach. They found a nice spot by the water, and they ate the poutine they had bought.

"Hey Bianca, can I talk to you for a sec?" Kassandra stared at the water.

"Yeah sure, give us a sec, Angel." Bianca got up and brushed off the sand grains from her bottom.

Angel nodded and continued to eat her poutine. Kassandra and Bianca entered the water; the cold water had them shivering, but they stuck their feet in the sand until they eventually became comfortable with the temperature.

"I want out, Bianca, and honestly, when you're ready... you need to get out too," Kassandra said, watching the birds fly across the lake.

"Where is this coming from?" Bianca looked at Kassandra. "You making bare gwop."

"I'm going to end up killing someone, Bianca. This thing inside of me is taking more control every time it's unleashed... one day I might lose full control." Kassandra looked down at her feet, wiggling her toes in the sand.

"It was a crazy night, I know, but out of how many times did you act it out?" Bianca pointed out.

"Enough to play with the Grim Reaper." Kassandra slowly turned to face Bianca.

Their eyes met and there was a moment of silence. Bianca sighed and looked down at the water.

"You're serious this time, aren't you?" Bianca said in an unhappy voice.

"I'm always here for you, just not in that aspect." Kassandra consoled Bianca, wrapping one of her arms around her.

"You'll be back, Kassandra. The money is good, and I know you love me." Bianca looked at Kassandra.

Kassandra let out a sigh and took her arm off her. They both walked back to Angel and Bianca sat down.

"I'm going to head out right now. I've got to help out mom." Kassandra picked up her stuff and hugged Angel and Bianca, before walking away.

"What's with your long face, missy?" Angel had approached Bianca, noticing that her mood changed.

"She'll come back, I'm not worried," Bianca said in a straight voice.

"You're creeping me out. What happened with you two?" Angel asked.

"She won't be away for long…. They always come back," Bianca smiled.

"Okay, you're creeping me out," Angel backed away.

Bianca smiled and continued to watch the water….

Underestimating the resilience of Kassandra….

Years had passed, and Kassandra continued to go in and out in what she did, out of the love she had for the girls, yet only these few stories of Kassandra were shared with you. Her story had twists and turns that had made her feel hopeless at times. People had given up on her and she was told she would not be saved. The few people, including Aisha, stayed by her side, and continued to hear her cries and send prayers. Bianca ended up moving out of the country after years of saving up, and Kassandra eventually lost contact with her and the other girls. Eventually, with faith like a mustard seed, Kassandra finally walked out of the cycle to fulfill other paths that are destined for her.

The straight to the point update is that Kassandra finally put Diablo to rest. She did the impossible and became a motivational speaker, getting involved in ministries and providing staff educational workshops that deal with this population. As this chapter of her story ended, may Kassandra continue to reap the blessings she sowed.

Hood Affair

Ngozi got off the phone and placed it by a nearby plastic stool. She tied up her hair into a messy bun and sank into the warm bath. She only had an hour to get ready, and she wanted to enjoy treating herself with a bath, champagne and eating strawberries. After 20 minutes, she got up and rinsed herself. Putting on some mango shea butter on her skin, she put on her favourite black short-sleeved shirt and black booty shorts. She put her hair back into a ponytail and put on a gold heart necklace that was gifted to her. She brushed and flossed her teeth before popping a peppermint gum.

Ngozi was excited to go out tonight. She put on her white Gucci sandals that were also gifted to her and got out of the house. She was walking on the street when she heard music blasting from around the corner and felt the sound waves ripple throughout her body. A grey Range Rover turned in, and the tinted windows rolled down, with the music continuing to play at full volume. She smiled and got into the passenger seat, and they drove off to the other end of the town. The car finally turned into a secluded area by the beach, and the music was turned down low. She got out and hopped in the back and waited for her lover to join her.

"Hey babe, miss me?" Ricardo said into Ngozi's ear softly with his husky voice, before kissing her neck gently, making her pearl ripe for picking.

"Yes, daddy," Ngozi answered before kissing Ricardo passionately.

Ricardo was the product of a Brazilian father and Congolese mother, with smooth bronze skin tone and a beautiful set of dark brown eyes. He looked like he could model in multiple posters and videos without even trying. He just had this captivating look that drew attention from all corners.

They continued to talk and laugh throughout the night and went to a drive-through to grab some food before driving to an empty parking lot to eat. Ricardo offered her some gum after they were eating and continued to talk about random things. Ngozi suddenly brought up the "What were they?" question. Ricardo's body language was tense before he let out a big sigh.

"I don't want to be in a serious relationship with you, because I don't want either side to get hurt," Ricardo looked at Ngozi, frowning, "but I want us to move in together. I want you to have my baby."

"You're not making any sense at all, Ricardo. You are confusing me and I'm not having…" he pulled Ngozi into him and kissed her. She tried to finish her sentence, but his lips were pressed against her, smothering all words. She was so frustrated with this man; he didn't want to make it official, yet he wanted her all for himself. Every time she tried to distance herself, he always found a way to get in contact with her – through reappearing near Sheridan or Yorkdale Mall, through collect calls or getting one of his boys to keep her updated with what's going on. He even had her full name tattooed on the front of his right arm. She just wanted it to be all over and to move on with her life, to find someone who could appreciate her and cherish her, and to eventually build a life with her as husband and wife. But it takes two to mingle, so she partially – well actually, mostly – blamed herself for this soul tie.

Ngozi returned the kiss and could feel Ricardo smile as he remained victorious; he had won once again. His hand began to fondle her full breasts under her black t-shirt, before finally exposing her soft, warm, gold olive skin. She fell into a trance by his intoxicating hands, his fingers tracing her figure down to her pants eager to plunge into her wetness. Suddenly the phone rang, and Ricardo quickly put himself back into his "business" mode. As he got out of his car to pick up the call, Ngozi let out a sigh of relief.

"Whew, that was close," Ngozi said to herself as she fixed herself up and sat patiently, while Ricardo was pacing back and forth. This was the norm when it came to them hanging out: Ricardo would have multiple flip phones that would ring nonstop. She never asked him, but she had an idea that the line of work he was in was far from normal.

Flashback to 4 years ago...

Ricardo and Ngozi had met at a Latin club somewhere around North York. She was peer pressured by her friends to go, and only agreed because it was a birthday and farewell party for a friend who would go back to El Salvador for two years. From the minute she stepped into the club, she walked straight towards a corner and sat, while her friends laughed and danced. She tried to stay out of the radar and was doing fine for the majority of the night, till someone took notice of her.

A man approached Ngozi and sat next to her before she could politely decline. He started to introduce himself with Ngozi looking down and positioning herself so she could face the opposite way. The man was telling her he goes by

50

Ferjal and was from Lebanon, and how he was studying and working in Canada in hopes he could become a citizen. *Oh great,* she thought, *another guy that wants to mooch off an unfortunate soul. Well, that girl ain't me,* she told herself as she attempted to get up. Ferjal grabbed Ngozi's hand and sat her right back down.

"I think you have me misunderstood. I like this country and I can take care of myself and you too." He looked into her eyes.

Ferjal reached into his pockets and pulled up a roll of 50-dollar bills and placed it in her hand. She looked at the cash in front of her, with Ferjal smirking, believing she would give in. Ngozi gradually looked at him and suddenly burst out howling with laughter.

"Who did you think I am? I'm sorry, sweetheart, I don't roll like that! Better luck next time!" She placed the money on the table and squeezed herself out to find her friends.

Ngozi reunited with her group of friends, as they shared their amusement of the story. She finally loosened up as she started to learn basic dance moves, while she was in the middle of her social circle.

"I need to go to the restroom, can you come with me, girl?" her friend Hazel asked.

"Yeah, of course, I need to use it myself," Ngozi volunteered.

They were navigating the crowd and in the middle of the chaos, she bumped into a tall figure. "I'm so sorry, I hope I didn't…"

Ngozi was interrupted by the mysterious person. "No worries, Senorita," he said in a seductive husky voice.

Hazel grabbed Ngozi by the arm as they went into the washroom.

"He looks scrumptious," Hazel told Ngozi as she fixed her hair into a bun.

"He looks like trouble," Ngozi replied, though she agreed with Hazel.

"As if you never experienced that before. Remember CG?" Hazel shot back.

"Oh my goodness, you never let that go yet? It's been already two years, Hazel!" Ngozi rolled her eyes.

Flashback to 6 years ago...

CG was a former lover that was going on and off for the past three years before he got deported. CG was a Haitian American who had been trafficking cocaine from Colombia for years and had managed to connect with some bikers from Montreal. Later on, he made connections with some local triads in Toronto which had him making frequent trips between the two major cities. They met in the York University Observatory in one of their public openings, and they had been caught up in an intense situation-ship. They remained in contact here and there since his deportation, but that chapter is closed. Ngozi wasn't about to get involved in another urban thriller for herself again.

Ngozi had an admiration and attraction for the hustlers and shottas, but she would rather keep her distance from them. She would rather have them at arm's length as acquaintances, while she has a future with someone who had a steady career. Yet, when she turned 21, all she had been attracting were bad boys. Even the same ones that wouldn't take the chance to express their feelings were starting to make their moves.

Back to 4 years ago...

Yet here was this mystery man who stirred butterflies in her stomach. *Probably won't see him again,* Ngozi thought as the girls went back outside. They continued to enjoy the rest of the night until it was time to go. They were hanging outside the establishment to wait for Hazel's older sister to pick them up, when suddenly she felt a strong grip on her wrist. She turned around and it was Ferjal. She used her free hand to claw Ferjal's hand.

"Can you let go of me please?!" Ngozi fought the urge to punch his face.

"Not until you give me a number," Ferjal tightened his grip.

Her heart started to beat fast as she tried to maintain self-control in this situation. She didn't want to escalate and cause any unnecessary drama, but she wanted to reach for the sharpest object and jook out his eyeballs.

"I'm not going to repeat myself again. Let... me... GO!" Ngozi started to raise her voice, in hopes that it would cause Ferjal to back off.

"Okay, let me help myself in getting that number…." Ferjal tried to reach for Ngozi's phone, until a big hand grabbed his shoulder. Ngozi could feel the pressure being used that caused Ferjal to let go of his grip and get on his knees.

"Relax there, buddy, I didn't know she was with you!" Ferjal pleaded.

It was the mysterious man, and all Ngozi could think of was trying to walk away before she had to owe him for being the "knight in shining armour." Yet she was getting a bit turned on by the man's strength, plus she contemplated sneaking a kick at Ferjal's balls.

"You should have just respected her, even if she wasn't with anyone," the man said as he continued to tighten his grip.

Okay that was hot. She trembled in disgust at that thought. *I think it's time to go,* she thought as she turned around, urging her friends to leave the scene.

POP!!!

Ngozi's bad knee gave out and she hit the ground, while all her friends ran to her aid. *Not now,* she prayed, as she used the support from her friends and hauled herself back up. *Good, my knee didn't give out completely this time.* She sighed in relief, but shock on the knee was making her walk crippled. *I need to rest for a bit,* Ngozi thought, but was hesitant with her surroundings. Her friends sat her down by a nearby bench in a bus shelter while she massaged her knee.

"You okay?" Hazel asked with a concerned look on her face.

"I'll be fine, just need to put ice on it to prevent it from swelling too much," Ngozi reassured her friend.

"Let's get you a cab," Hazel suggested.

There goes my one-dollar oyster date night with myself. Ngozi dreaded in her mind about the cost of the taxi fare.

"Are you okay, beautiful?" The mysterious man appeared out of nowhere. He looked concern for Ngozi's well-being.

Not again, she thought. *He just knows when to show up.* She rolled her eyes but put on a half-smile.

"Yes, I'm fine, I just need to get home ASAP." She just wanted him to go away.

But the man did not budge, and Ngozi glared at her friends for help.

"Do you have a ride, ladies?" the man asked.

Before Ngozi could nod her head or lie, Hazel shook her head. *This woman... always wanting to add on more to the nonsense.* Ngozi was in disbelief.

"Thank you, but we are waiting for our ride," Ngozi jumped in.

"I can offer you ladies a ride," the man replied, "or help out with the cost."

"Well, of course," Hazel replied. "It's probably 200 or 300 for all of us, Ngozi lives far from us but the rest of us live fairly close."

I'm going to manhandle this girl, Ngozi mumbled to herself and tried to get up, but her knee refused to cooperate.

"No problem, I'll give extra, but I don't mind giving your girl a ride." He looked at Ngozi.

"We left together so we are going to go home together," Ngozi answered in a stern voice.

"Do you mind giving us a sec?" Hazel stepped in using her index finger and thumb finger to form the "ok" sign.

"Sure, you can hold on to this and make up your mind," the man said, as he handed Ngozi a stack of cash. "If I don't see you again, it was a pleasure to meet all of you." He smiled and gave the girls some space, while lighting up a Cuban cigar.

The girls hovered around Ngozi and Hazel, taking the stack from her and started counting the bills.

"550, 650, 750... 1550.... This man dropped us two grand!!" Hazel exclaimed before trying to stop herself. She turned around to see if he had heard them, but he seemed to be focused on being on his phone.

"That's more than enough to take us all home and for us to split the profit, Hazel," Ngozi sighed.

"And if you keep in touch with him it'll be a lifetime supply, duhhh," Hazel said in a matter-of-fact voice.

"Look, I don't have my shit on me and we don't even know this man at all." Ngozi took in a deep breath to calm herself down. "I'm not getting in the car. This man tried to pull some shady stunt and I can't even defend myself." She looked at him and assessed him. "He could easily overpower me, and I'll be lucky if all he does is touch me up," Ngozi looked at her friends.

"I'll sneak a picture of him and the car so if shit goes down, we got chu," Hazel came back with her response.

"And what happens if he takes me to a pig farm?" Ngozi asked.

"Huh, what does a pig farm have to do with anything?" Hazel looked confused.

"Not going to get into details," Ngozi replied.

"How about we do a sleepover to save money. Is that good enough?" Hazel proposed.

"I'm not going, Hazel!" Ngozi clenched her teeth to stop herself from exploding. she was on the verge of just going back home by herself, but she took a few deep breaths before glaring at Hazel.

"Okay, okay, fine, the least we can do is to thank him and say bye, sheesh… your head is as hard as a coconut." Hazel had finally given in.

Hazel pouted as a last resort to gain pity, but it was to no avail. She slouched and walked slowly to the man. Everyone watched as Hazel played with her hair and looked sad about bringing him the news. The man laughed and walked with her back to the group. *Now what on earth did this woman tell the boy this time?* Ngozi rolled her eyes and sighed, before trying to not give them a deadly cut eye.

"As long as you girls are safe, that's all that matters." The man smiled.

At least he is not being a jerk about it, Ngozi thought.

"Although it would have been nice to be acquainted," he added.

Well, so much for that thought. She put on a super fake smile. She wanted him to feel he was unwanted. *Please don't make this any more difficult.*

"I feel bad for taking your money," Ngozi wanted to give back the stash. *That way he can pull no tricks,* she thought as she wanted to cover any possible slip ups.

The man smiled and replied, "No worries, sweetheart, this is just chump change. Plus, I believe if it was meant to be, it would have happened, right?"

Ngozi motioned for Hazel to call a cab. When it stopped in front of the club, the man helped the girls walk Ngozi into the cab. Just when they were about to leave, Hazel and the other girls waved while Ngozi just gave a quick nod to thank him. The man just smiled and walked the other way.

Flashback to 2 years ago...

It had been two years after that encounter and Hazel would bring it up randomly just for Ngozi to dismiss it. Deep down she was a bit curious about the mystery man, but she brushed it off as a once in a lifetime encounter and continued on with her daily life.

58

On one evening during the summer, she wanted to treat herself or have a girl's night out. She wanted to go to a popular all-you-can-eat steakhouse up by Woodbridge. She called up Hazel to see if she was down to go. Hazel told Ngozi to give her about half an hour to get ready. Ngozi quickly hopped into the shower and put on a low-cut ruby-red dress, with a thigh-high slit on the right side. She put on a pair of white-wedge sandals, and she had also straightened her hair. She waited patiently for Hazel to come pick her up.

Hazel pulled in with her pickup truck. She was wearing a lavender-purple version of Ngozi's dress, with white stilettos, and she had glossy curls.

"Look at you... I see someone is starting to dress up," Hazel smirked.

"Oh hush, I'm going back to baggy pants and hoodies after this," Ngozi kissed her teeth, while she got into the truck. "Heels, dress and pickup truck," she chuckled.

"Yup, gotta let folks knows we ain't playing around and we like it big and rough," Hazel replied and stuck her tongue out.

Rush hour was ending, but there was a buildup of traffic, so they just killed time by blasting Hip Hop, Soca and Dancehall and singing at the top of their lungs. Hazel had this need for speed and raced whoever she wanted to, while Ngozi was holding on to the car roof handle for her dear life.

They finally turned into the steakhouse and got nice seating outside on the patio. They both ordered tequilas, mojitos and peach bellinis, and waited for the waiters to bring in all kinds of meat to the table. Both of the girls went to pick up some side dishes to complement the richness of the meat. Later on, there was a spectacular dance performance as well as musicians; it was a lively night for sure. The alcohol was kicking in, and the girls started to crack jokes and pull pranks on each other.

"I feel so turnt," Hazel said as she took in two more tequila shots.

"Drink more water and piss it out my girl," Ngozi laughed at Hazel, almost knocking over her water glass.

"I need to smoke," Hazel changed the topic and was searching in her purse. She pulled out a vape pen and was dangling it out in front of her.

"Can we like get out of here and go to a park or go to your place?" Ngozi had to get Hazel sober now, if they were ever going to leave.

"Oh fine," Hazel pouted as she put the pen back, and went to chug a glass of water.

"I need to go pee pee," Hazel laughed as she excused herself from the table.

Ngozi chuckled as she drank some water to start diluting the potency from the drinks.

"I guess it was meant to be, madame." A husky voice sent shivers down Ngozi's spine.

Why does this voice sound so familiar? She tried to figure out who it was and started to look around. When she got up to turn the other way, the same man she met years ago at the club walked up to the side of the seats and gave her a radiating smile.

"I guess someone was having a blast here," the man looked at the pile of fruits and meat on the plates. "I hope I'm not disturbing your date night." He looked around to make sure he wasn't going to be ambushed.

Ngozi shrugged and said, "Girls' night out and we have big appetites."

"Ooooo, what do I see here?" Hazel had an evil smile and was walking towards them.

Talk about perfect timing. Ngozi knew it was going to be a long night, and Hazel for sure wasn't going to let this go anytime soon.

"Hope I'm not invading your space and time, ladies, but I had to say hi," the man said.

"Of course not. If you not with anyone you should come join us," Hazel quickly offered, feeling the wrath of Ngozi unfold with each word.

"You sure?" the man asked while observing the ladies' eye exchange.

"Oh no, no, no, if you don't mind us stuffing our mouths before we get the bill," Hazel answered with a big smile.

The man looked at Ngozi again for her consent, and she pulled out an empty chair on the side. "You free to join," Ngozi offered. She didn't want to go back and forth with

Hazel, and she secretly wanted to know why they would bump into each other again.

"Why thank you so much, I'm humbled." The man sat right next to Ngozi.

Turns out there was more to this man than some good-looking rich jock, and they quickly got acquainted and found more things in common. From exchanging their names to conversations about their heritage, medicine, history, politics, nature and law - down to cracking up jokes while the girls finished everything on their plates - which led to Ngozi letting out her finale burp that impressed him.

"Bravo! Bravo!!" Ricardo applauded, while Ngozi got up and bowed.

"Why thank you, thank you very much." She put her hands on her hips and was proud.

Hazel was finally sober enough to drive, and the girls asked for their waiter to get the bill.

"It's on me," Ricardo got up and followed the waiter, and insisted that the girls sit down.

"My goodness!" Hazel exclaimed. "He's generous as fuck." She looked at Ngozi.

Ricardo came back, then both of the girls got up, and they went to walk towards the parking lot. He whistled when he saw Hazel's ride. "She's a beauty, didn't know these bad boys were your type." He gave Hazel the nod of approval.

"Oh why, because I'm a woman?" Hazel gave Ricardo a "mhm" look.

"Oh no, don't take it the wrong way, Hazel," Ricardo laughed, "I should have known better after having that wonderful talk at the restaurant. Please forgive me." He took one of Hazel's hands and kissed it.

Hazel blushed and winked at Ngozi, while Ngozi gave her the side eye.

"I should let you ladies get going now. It was fun hanging out and we should do it another time." Ricardo reached for a piece of paper and pen to write down his number.

"Oooo old school, I like I like," Hazel whispered to Ngozi when he handed her the paper.

"Take care and hit me up sometime." Ricardo reached for Ngozi's hand and kissed it before he left.

Throughout the car ride, Hazel kept talking about the night, while Ngozi was zoned out looking at the city lights. After they reached Hazel's place, the girls took turns pulling on the vape pen. Eventually they passed out on the couches, and that night that would lead Ngozi into a spiral of events before reaching the ultimate deal breaker.

Ricardo got back in the car, and Ngozi was just playing with her fingers.

"Hey love, have to meet up with a couple of folks, but I can drop you off if you don't want to join." Ricardo kissed her on the forehead.

"It's fine, I'll join you," she saw Ricardo grinning before she looked out the window.

They started driving through the back roads slowly while Ricardo was doing all sorts of things – answering his pagers and calls, grabbing random bottles and bags – yet Ngozi never thought too deep into it. They finally hit a major intersection, and he made a sharp turn and continued south. She was just in her own zone, so she didn't notice that he kept glancing at the rear-view mirror. They were approaching a stoplight and there were only four seconds left, when Ricardo reached under the seats and pulled up a small plastic bag.

"Hold this for me, baby," Ricardo told Ngozi as he placed the bag with unknown contents into her palm and put his hand on top of hers. They made a full stop at the red light, when she slid her hand away from his to open her palm to examine the mysterious white crystals.

"Huh!" Ngozi exclaimed as she lifted the bag up and looked closer.

"Yo watch it!" Ricardo said in a stern voice. He quickly used his hand to cover her hand, right before a cruiser rolled up next to them at the light. "Look straight and chill out," he whispered to Ngozi.

He didn't have to because she realized what the crystals were and was in a state of shock. *This motherfucker trying to set me up!* Ngozi started to fume as her heartbeat quickened its pace. But she had to put on a poker face and acting skills so the cops wouldn't notice a thing.

Luckily, just before the officer started to look, the light turned green, and Ricardo drove the car like a perfectionist following all the traffic rules and was sparking conversation with Ngozi. She talked back to relax her tense muscles, but she needed to give Ricardo a piece of her mind. The cruiser continued to follow behind, until he made a turn into a small street and the cruiser drove past them. Ngozi continued to control her breathing to calm her heart, while Ricardo found a hidden place and turned off the car so it would camouflage.

"Whew, that was a close one," he nervously chuckled. "Whoa, what's up with that grimy look?" he stuttered as Ngozi glared at him.

"You son of a bitch! You tried to set me up!! How dare you!!!" She tried to not raise her voice to wake up everyone.

"What the hell are you talking about?" Ricardo shot back.

"This, Ricardo." Ngozi dangled the bag up in his face.

"Whoa whoa, chill out." He went to grab it out of her hand. "Do you know how much that's worth?!" Ricardo held the bag like it was his lifeline.

"My fucking freedom – you dirt bag." Ngozi was so tempted to spit at him.

"C'mon ma, why you trippin'? You know I'm in the game." He leaned in to kiss her. Ngozi put out her hand to stop him midway. Ricardo backed up, appalled by her action.

"It's one thing to do your shit and it's another thing trying to force me into being your guinea pig without my consent." Ngozi glared at him. She wanted to reach under her seat and show him she would rather go in for a better reason.

Ricardo must have sensed her intention, because he grabbed her hands and looked at her. "Look, I need to put food on the table and no one would hire a person like me." He took a deep breath to control his temper. "I know you a rider, and I even trust you to hold this work without ratting me out…. you love me, don't you?" Ricardo didn't break his eye contact with her.

"I'm not one of your bitches…. It would have been different if you were my baby dad or husband, because I would have known and gave consent to the consequences. You fully telling me some bullshit earlier and expecting there'll be no catch for pulling this stunt." She pulled her hands back and crossed them. "Doesn't work like that…. now you owe me a favour for this fuckery." Ngozi glared at him.

Then she put on a wicked grin; she couldn't allow Ricardo to see her being vulnerable. She was hurt that he would see her as some kind of mule. But she should have known better and blamed herself for her being so naive. Even the way he put it earlier that night, he wanted to create this messed up situation to manipulate her.

"Tsk tsk tsk, at least we can establish our business relationship, right, Ricardo?" Ngozi continued to speak as Ricardo face continued to tense up. "We can both exchange favours from now on." She smiled as she pulled up one of her old flip phones. "I do apologize for me snapping. Let's just say we're even right now… to have a new start… partner." Her smile stretched until it could not reach any further.

There was no response from Ricardo. Their car ride back would have been awkward if he hadn't put in his

66

Reggaeton/Hip Hop CD in the car player. They kept seeing patrol cars around. Ngozi later found out there had been a major raid operation in the area. When he dropped her off, he tried apologizing again and she just apologized for her overreacting and to just leave it at that.

Ngozi didn't even bother taking her clothes off and just sat in the bed. *Why did I even trip out like that? It's not like I was clueless.... Maybe I should make it up for coming at him... no, he should have just been upfront with me... but then again, maybe he had the right to do what he did.* She kept arguing with herself while she stared at his contact on her phone. *There's always gon be some next chick who's down and would be down for that... I mean I'm another broad in his eyes... I wouldn't be so mad if he just giving me a heads up.... No, he's conditioning me... why is this even up for debate?* She tapped the side of her head real hard to knock some sense into it.

She felt her tears trickling down and was so confused as to why she was acting like a punk. She went to the fridge to grab a bottle of Appleton and took a couple of big gulps before heading to bed. She couldn't sleep at all until the sun came out, and the liquor finally made her drowsy enough that she gradually closed her eyes.

The phone vibrated a few times before Ngozi managed to open her eyes. She thought it was Ricardo. *Oh, it's only Hazel.* She was half relieved and disappointed.

"Yo trick, what happen to you?" Hazel asked,

"Long ass night, don't even really want to talk about it," Ngozi mumbled. She could feel her head pounding.

"Did you watch the news? They caught Ricardo with all sorts of goodies! He ain't gon be coming out anytime soon, that's for sure!!" Hazel exclaimed.

"Wait, what?!" Ngozi forced herself to get up and go turn on her TV in the living room. She just watched the screen without blinking when they kept showing his picture on repeat, while the reporter brought up the different charges the group would be pressed for.

"Did you know this trifling ass was with three other hoes too, and they are trying to claim they didn't know, and he set them up! Haha, so stupid!!" Hazel laughed but Ngozi didn't join in.

"Motherfucker could probably sneak a whole entire key in their purses, and they wouldn't know." Hazel laughed even louder. "Yo N, you good? ... Aww don't feel no ways about this fool. He already got his karma for tryna be a playa and look at him! All the hoodrats he trying to sleep with turned on him." Hazel attempted to comfort her.

Hazel had no clue that she would have needed to come get Ngozi out if that officer decided to stop the car last night. Ngozi slouched on the couch. *That was too close for comfort.* She told Hazel she'll call her back and she went to kneel at the edge of her bed. She closed her eyes and started to pray, "Lord, I don't know what on earth I got myself into, but You continue to protect me and I thank You once again, just like the countless times You watched over me. I do pray for Ricardo and may you protect him also.... I don't have the words to say but I trust in You to know my heart... In Jesus' name we pray, Amen." Ngozi got up and laid in her bed.

Many months had passed and Ngozi found herself travelling for a few hours to reach her destination. It had been a lengthy process, but she finally got clearance. After going through being searched and patiently waiting, she sat down and looked at the glass pane. She waited for the door to open and for this muscular figure sit right in front of her and pick up a phone. She took a deep breath and picked up her end of the phone.

"Hope all is well with you," she said as she was making little eye contact.

"Yeah, I'm surprised to be honest... never thought I would see you anytime soon," the figure replied.

"Just wanted to make sure that you alright, Ricardo.... I still have a heart," Ngozi replied.

And then there was a silence that no words could describe....

To be Continued...

In Memory of Gaza

GD (Till We Meet Again)

"Excuse me, I was wondering where 666 is located. It should've been around here, but I don't see it," Shonda asked a passing caretaker. She had spent 15 minutes walking around the cemetery and had no luck finding her friend.

"Oh, sometimes the ground swallows up the markers," the caretaker replied, as he started tapping around the area between two headstones. "Ah, there it is, let me dig it up for you." He plunged his shovel straight into the earth and pulled up a stained and rusted grave marker out of the ground.

Shonda was in disbelief about its condition and kept a steady gaze at the gravesite while struggling to give her thanks to the man as he continued his duties. Once the man was out of sight, she allowed her tears to trickle down her cheeks into the ground.

"I'm so sorry that I took so long. I would've come sooner but..." Shonda fought her sobs. "I didn't know... I didn't want to believe what I heard." She took a handkerchief out of her jean pockets and walked towards a leaking water hose close by the grave. She wet the handkerchief and went to the grave and gently wiped the marker till most of the build-up was gone. She put down her red handbag and took out a big spliff, a red lighter and a big bottle of Hennessy. Shonda poured half of the bottle onto the grave before taking three big gulps, then she started to smoke.

"If it wasn't for you, this would be my home.... I can't thank you enough, GD"

Those words instantly sparked her flashback to when she was a freshman in high school. Shonda was a brilliant woman, anyone could see that, and wouldn't doubt her for a second. But the issue was that she was not showing it in the academic aspect; she didn't really care for school. She was constantly skipping classes to sneak into college and universities and walk into any lectures she could managed to get away with.

She also loved to explore places since she was a child, and at that particular time in her life, going to different neighbourhoods in the GTA became something of interest to her. One night, while walking around a well-known neighbourhood in the core of downtown, Shonda was approached by a group of men who had taken notice of her. Outnumbering her and carrying objects, they mocked Shonda as they stalked behind her, making derogatory remarks. Shonda was too focused on speed-walking that she didn't realize she had become cornered in a dead end. Her memories became blurry as they pulled out shiny objects, demanding which set she repped. Shonda usually would not entertain this type of nonsense, but feeling restrained had her attitude flare up, as she talked back, provoking and enticing them to go to the full extent with her.

Shonda started to prepare for the fight of her life – she was not going down without taking one of them with her to the Duat. Shonda raised her fists ready to take blows as the boys continued to mock her. She closed her eyes, ready to

71

swing, not noticing a tall figure had appeared from the shadows and tapped on one of the boy's shoulders.

"What did I tell you boys about picking on ladies. Move from here and fucking put in real work." A deep voice had Shonda peeking through her eyes.

"Fam, she was just walking up and down the street like her shit don't stink," one of the boys decided to speak up.

"Do I have to repeat myself?" the man sounded agitated.

"No, no fam, heard you loud and clear, we gon cut," one of the boys responded quickly and Shonda heard shoes scattering. She opened her eyes fully to see who was this guardian angel that God sent.

"Thank you, sir." She looked at the pavement and didn't want to make eye contact due to the embarrassment.

"Why you out and about at this time young lady? Your family going to be worried sick." The man sounded puzzled.

"I was just looking around; I'm going to head home now." Shonda felt her cheeks burning up as she wanted to cut the conversation short. She continued to have her head down while pointing to the direction she thought a bus stop would be.

"The block is hot right now; I'll take you home. You can stay on the phone with a friend if it makes you feel any better," the man said. He could tell that Shonda was uncomfortable with the offer, which she should be. She nodded her head quickly and took her phone out and gripped it hard. They both walked until she saw a dark car with tinted windows at the far back of the parking lot. The car made a beeping sound as it unlocked, as he went to the passenger side to open the door for her. Shonda stood there, debating if she should take any more risks for the night. The man knew she was weighing her options and he sighed.

"It's getting late, ma'am, and I'm a very busy man. I understand you're not from here, so you don't know who I am, but I really don't want anything happen to you." The man leaned a bit forward as Shonda turned away.

"How about you text your friends my license plate," the man suggested.

Shonda looked at him and stood still. The man started to look around, and he noticed movement near the buildings. She felt her gut churning, and she decided to jump in the car. The man got into the driver's seat and turned the ignition on before backing up.

"You can drop me off at the closest station," she said, looking out the window while gripping her phone.

"I go by the name of Dwayne Douglas, but people know me as GD," the man finally identified himself.

Shonda turned her head, facing him with a surprised expression.

"Might as well break the ice," GD shrugged as he made his way out of the neighbourhood.

"You can drop me off at Jane and Wilson," she said.

"Take this," GD reached into his pocket and took out a stash of 50 and 20 dollars.

73

Shonda didn't flinch and just stared.

"Ma'am, just pay for a cab to go wherever you need to go when I drop you off." GD did not take his eyes off the road and placed the stash into Shonda's hand quickly.

"Thank you so much, but I don't know how to repay..." She was stuttering her words.

"Don't watch that, this is nothing," GD cut in, "but a nice girl like you can't be roaming like that." Shonda felt her cheeks blushing and looked back at the window.

For the next while, they drove without speaking, with the radio playing in the background.

"My name is Shonda," she broke the silence.

"Nice to meet you, Shonda," GD smiled.

"Thank you... for standing up for me," she said quietly.

"It's all good, these youngins need to stop that unnecessary bullshit before they pick on the wrong one," GD replied.

"Guess I need to cut down on my hood adventures," Shonda mumbled, hoping GD wouldn't catch on.

"Wait wait wait wait... Hood adventures... that's what stirred the commotion back there?" GD was amused and chuckled.

"Yeah, I guess I should stick to rivers and forests." Shonda wanted to crawl into a ball.

GD started to laugh; it wasn't a light laugh but full belly laughs. Shonda was dying of embarrassment, but she hoped that she wouldn't ever see him again.

They finally reached Jane and Wilson, and Shonda pointed to the Coffee Time. GD dropped her off and drove off, and she took a cab home.

Shonda laid in her bed with her eyes wide open; images of the gravesite kept replaying whenever she tried to close her eyes. *They really left him in the dirt.* She was in disbelief; GD would have hustled his back off to make sure all his people were given a proper burial. She could still remember that night. She was listening to instrumentals and writing poetry for her first showcase. She decided to check her social media and noticed a handful of people were asking who got shot in downtown. Something didn't feel right, but Shonda brushed it off. The next day she was chilling with a group of friends at a nearby park. It was a beautiful autumn day, and she was writing a story about seasons while her friends sketched, sang and danced.

Her phone was vibrating, and when she picked up the phone, she heard screaming and crying on the other line and she couldn't make out what her boy was trying to say. *They smoked him, my nigga dead* – those words continued to repeat in Shonda's head. She put her phone down and walked away, her ears muffed out the sounds of her concerned friends.

Shonda turned off her phone and got on the bus. Her head was spinning from this nightmare and she wanted to wake up. She got in the subway train and collapsed onto a vacant seat. She zoned out and stared blankly at the train door throughout the whole ride. She didn't even realize that she had missed her stop, until the train conductor told her that the train was going out of service. She was at the other end of the subway line and decided to just take the long way home. She went upstairs and got on a bus. To avoid losing her focus again, she turned on her phone and answered her texts and missed calls.

It had been months since her encounter with GD, and Shonda never went back to that neighbourhood since. One night, she couldn't sleep and decided to go to a 24/7 convenience store up the street. She walked in and grabbed some baked goods and a bottle of pop before going to the counter. She was looking for some loose change in her jacket when she heard a familiar voice from behind.

"Put her stuff with mine," GD told the cashier, and the cashier billed her stuff with his bag of chips.

Shonda turned around and started to turn red. *Oh no, I was hoping I wouldn't see him again.* She grabbed her stuff and gave her thanks before walking out of the store.

"Hey you, slow down!" GD shouted from the door. Shonda stopped and turned around as GD jogged to reach to her.

"What are you doing out so late, missy? On another hood adventure?" GD chuckled.

"I was hoping you forgot about that," Shonda replied, her face turning bright red.

GD laughed as Shonda shriveled up.

"What you doing in my ends, GD?" she asked.

"Just waiting on someone for some business, but I got hungry and went to grab some chips," GD answered as he opened the bag of chips and stuffed a handful of chips in his mouth. "Want some?" he offered with his mouth full. Shonda politely declined. "Your loss," he shrugged as he stuffed himself with more chips.

"Well, it was nice bumping into you again GD, but I gotta go home," she said as she started to walk away.

"I can walk with you. My whip at my boy's crib," GD said as he followed her.

"I'll be fine, GD, thanks," Shonda said as she quickened her pace.

GD matched up her speed-walking. "Oh no, no, no, I refuse to have a woman walk home by herself this late," he insisted. *Ugh, why is he so stubborn*, she thought, *I'll just go by Palisades and check Tia for the night.* Shonda got her phone and texted Tia to let her know what was going on. Tia texted back her approval and Shonda sighed in relief. *I can always count on Tia*, she smiled but quickly put her straight face on when she noticed GD was looking at her. They continued to walk until they reached the major intersection, and GD's phone rang. He stepped back and took the call.

"Well, business calls! Take care of yourself," GD said. Shonda waved back and was about to cross the light. He grabbed her hand and she turned around confused.

"Here, take my number." GD took Shonda's phone and called his phone from hers. He gave her phone back and sprinted in the opposite direction. *The nerve of this guy*! She stood and stared as GD made a sharp turn at a corner. Her phone vibrated as she saw a text from GD. She shook her head as she read the text, "Text when you get home, ma". She continued to shake her head as she made her way to her friend's place.

Shonda was looking at prices on the cemetery's website. *Why is it so expensive to die?* she questioned as she saw the costs. She had become restless for a week now, and she wanted to return all the favours GD had done for her out of his good heart. She was looking for discounts and started working to save up her money.

Shonda spent nights contacting GD's old clique, but everyone seemed to not be able to help. *Or they don't want to*, she thought to herself. Instead, his boys informed her what the streets were saying, and she did not like what she was hearing. From drug deals gone wrong, to unresolved beefs and other mumbo jumbo. *Why is everyone so concerned with all these rumours while their boy's existence is being swallowed up in the earth?* She got off the phone with one of his boys before she cussed them off. *It's pointless,* Shonda thought as she went back to her bed and closed her eyes.

Shonda and GD's friendship continued to grow as they spent more time together, hanging by the lakeshore, late nights talking about life. GD taught Shonda a lot about the game, while she listened and took in the knowledge. She never wanted to get involved and he wouldn't allow it, even if she nagged him for the rest of their days. GD wanted Shonda to stay out of any mix up, so he would keep some things to himself, but he knew deep down that she knew what was going on, but would pretend nothing happened, which he was grateful for. He wanted to make sure that she could defend herself if anything should happen to him.

When GD got in trouble and got locked up, Shonda made sure his canteen was filled, and she was relaying messages between him and his family and friends. She visited him and was taking his collect calls often to make sure he was well. GD contacted and picked Shonda up the same night he got out; they went by the lakeshore and went for a stroll along the boardwalk in silence.

"I don't get why these kids want to be caught up so bad. It's so lonely at times." GD was looking at the illuminating rising moon. It looked so beautiful to him. He never noticed the roundness and perfection of the full moon before, but on this occasion, it stood out. Since it was so huge, he could see the dark spots, but to him it was like nature's beauty marks. They walked to a nearby bench and sat down, staring and admiring the night sky.

"You are one of the realest, Shonda. Not many people like me get that kind of blessing," GD continued as Shonda looked at a spider by a warning sign, spinning a perfect web, not common in the city.

"Burying my niggas, mans snaking each other, sometimes these fiends, I think about at times, but I continue to do it... it's fucked up," GD said. She could feel the pain in his voice as he reminisced.

"What's keeping you in it?" Shonda diverted her attention from the spider and looked at GD. *He got set back a little, but she was sure he would be back on his feet in no time,* she thought. "Once you settle back down again, you can start making smart investments, so eventually you can get out of the game and try to live a normal life for the rest of your days," she said innocently.

GD gave a slight chuckle at her remark. Shonda wasn't wrong but she didn't see the whole picture. He had been hustling since he was a child to support his struggling family and had only gotten more involved as he got older. Now it was to the point of no return, and he realized that he didn't even want to leave the game. He knew he could easily get out with the profit he was making but he always wanted more, even on nights he barely got out alive as a marked man – he would keep low and then picked up his business.

He almost left everything when one day in his corner, he saw a long-time partner-in-crime huddle in a cardboard box with some dirty towels as a mattress and blanket. This person used to sell rocks with GD on the block and was better in investing than him; the man had his own house and was using the profit to further his education. *Broke one of the crack commandments,* he thought as he stared at him in pity mixed with disgust. The man must have recognized GD, because he started begging and shaking his worn out hat with change to purchase some product. GD backed off and cussed him out and walked away before losing his cool and had nightmares about that encounter.

"It's not as easy as you think, Shonda. I have been doing this all my life and this is all I know," GD replied.

"I'm sure you can!" Shonda protested. "You got the brains of a technician, doctor, banker and even a teacher and mentor!" she exclaimed matter-of-factly, while using her fingers to count the different career paths GD could take with his intelligence.

"What am I going to do with you, kid," GD laughed as he wrapped his arm around Shonda's neck and pulled her close to him as he gave her a noogie.

"Hey, hey, you messing up my hair." Shonda managed to wrestle away GD's grip, and fixed her hair, while giving him a glare as he continued to chuckle.

"You know what I admire about you, Shonda?" GD's amused face started to soften up as he looked at her. "No matter what you've been through or how wicked a person is, you can still see the good in them and still bring joy for yourself, even though the world would have given up a long time ago." He looked down at his shoes.

Then there was silence once again as the waves and seagulls sang their song.

"Don't ever change that, homie. I'll be damned if I ever cause you to be cold hearted," GD said to break the silence.

Shonda woke up from her restless sleep; her first major event she had to prepare for, and she was exhausted. *Pull it together, Shonda,* she scolded herself as she hopped into the shower to wake her body up. She rinsed her face in the shower and allowed the water to drench her hair in the process.

She started to recite her performance while fighting the temptation to stay at home and cry in her bed.

You got this. GD would have given you an ass whooping if he saw you like this, Shonda tried to cheer herself up. GD couldn't bear to watch his people wanting to quit, though she thought his tough love was a little harsh at times, but he would show a softer side and talk it out.

She got into her elegant black dress and went over her poetry book to make sure all the pieces she was going to share were bookmarked. She opened the drawer and traced her finger inside until she pulled out a black jewelry box.

Shonda took a deep breath as she sat at the edge of the bed with the box in front of her. Opening the box very slowly, she went to mirror to see how it would look on her.

Shonda and GD hadn't hung out for quite some time, because Shonda took on some offers for her art and work that required her to travel to different parts of the country. GD was driving her in the beginning, but she didn't want him to spend too much money, so he began to focus on making more money for himself.

It was about a month and a half before GD got murdered, and Shonda had begun making a vision board for a novel she had been writing since she was young. Her phone rang and she smiled when she heard GD's voice on the other line.

"What you saying right now," he asked.

"Nothing much, I'm just working on my table of contents for my project," Shonda replied.

"Do you have some time to chill for a bit?" GD asked.

"Yeah of course, I haven't seen you for so long! We got to catch up," she exclaimed.

"I'll be downstairs in 3," GD said, and he hung up the phone before Shonda could say goodbye to him.

"Ugh, this guy." She shook her head as she started to get ready.

Shonda sat on the front step and waited until she could feel loud music from a distance. She saw GD's car make a sharp turn, and she got up as he parked his car at her front entrance.

"I feel sorry for your tires, homie, and what am I going to tell my mom about the tire marks?" Shonda stared at the dark lines on the road.

"Just tell her you were testing out your painting skills," GD said, smirking at his dry joke.

"Soooo funny," Shonda rolled her eyes as she got into the car and GD pressed on his gas.

They drove for about two hours up north and Shonda couldn't remember when she dozed off, but she woke up when she felt the car stop and saw a big welcome sign.

"Eummm, where are we?" she asked, as she looked around and saw only a few cars and a forest.

"I been wanting to go here and thought I should bring you alone since you love nature and all," GD answered.

They both got out of the car. GD grabbed a huge backpack and stretched before walking past the sign. There were a few bulletin boards on both sides, some with trail maps and some with information about different species of plants and animals. They took the time to look over them and GD saw Shonda's face glow in fascination.

"Oh my gosh, this is the conservation I always talk about!" Shonda said with glee.

"Yeah, I looked into it and I wanted to come check it out," GD replied as they picked a nice trail that would lead into the marshlands.

They walked alongside the path and admired the songs of different birds, while Shonda tried to distinguish each sound of the birds. GD was more interested in the insects, and Shonda was amazed by how many different species he could identify.

"I didn't know you were into this sort of stuff that deeply," Shonda said.

"Yeah, you probably thought the only science I cared about was chemistry, didn't you," GD laughed.

"You and your comments," she rolled her eyes as they continue to walk, until they found a huge log that was close by the marshland.

They sat on the log and watched the herons fly in and out of the waters. Shonda kept going to the edge to catch enormous dragonflies and frogs and studied them closely.

GD pulled out mini hand sanitizer bottles so she could clean her hands after she was completely done. When she finally exhausted herself and sat down, he pulled out two water bottles and gave one to her.

"Hey hey hey, don't drown on me, little girl! Slow downnnn," GD cautioned as Shonda chugged all the water with huge gulps.

"Ahhhhh," she rubbed her belly and let out a huge burp that caused some of the birds to fly away. "Excuse me," Shonda smiled as GD just stared at her in disbelief.

"At least that hit the spot," he shrugged as he took a few sips of his bottle.

Shonda looked at the clear blue sky with few white clouds with admiration, while GD looked for something inside his bag.

"This is one of the gifts I wanted to give you, Shonda," he said, and she turned to look at him.

GD pulled out a black leather notebook with a beautiful handmade embossed lotus flower and the words "Renewed Journey" on it. Shonda's jaw dropped wide open as he placed the book in her hands and smiled.

"I hope you like it. Took me ages to get this done, and you might want to close your mouth before the frogs think you competing with them for a meal," GD smiled.

Shonda ran her fingers on the surface and traced the design. She opened it and saw a gold cross necklace and a handwritten message. She read it silently:

Dedicated to Shonda,

Thank you for your friendship and cheerful spirit! You don't know how much your joy shed light into the darkness I grew up in. I wanted to show my appreciation for everything that you have done, and I know how much you love writing so I made this for you. I hope you also love the cross I got. I know how much faith means to you and it also inspired me too! May you continue to pursue your gift and passion.

Cheers,

Dwayne Douglas

Shonda's eyes started to glitter as her emotions began to build up; she couldn't take her eyes off her gift. GD grew concerned with her silence. *Does she like it? Is my lotus too ugly?* His mind was going a mile a minute.

Shonda turned to him and hugged him so tight that GD didn't know how to react and looked around to see if any bystanders were around.

"Thank you so much, sooooo muchhh!" Shonda kept repeating to GD.

"I wanted to make sure I gave this to you, you know... in case if anything happens," he spoke quietly.

Shonda suddenly got up and gave GD the death glare.

"What are you talking about!" she demanded.

"Whoa, relax, Shonda, I'm just saying that 'cause you may never know," he answered.

"You being extra nice and friendly all of a sudden with these thoughtful gifts and then you make these kind of 'what if' remarks! What are you not telling me, GD?" Shonda said in a stern voice.

"God damn, you starting to sound like my mother. I can't do anything nice for women without being interrogated," GD sighed.

"You're not answering me," Shonda continued to press on.

GD started to laugh. "Look, nothing is going on. I was just thinking of all the people I really care about and I never get the chance to show how much they mean to me," he answered.

Shonda continued to stare to probe for more information, but she could see the sincerity in his eyes and hear that he was genuine. She decided not to question him any further, which would later haunt her in the near future.

The sun was starting to sink low and the mosquitoes started to make a feast out of the both of them, so they speed-walked back to the car and made the long drive back home.

"I'm really happy to have known you, Shonda," GD said.

"I'm happy to have met you too, but you have been practically saying that the whole day," Shonda answered back.

"I know, and I can never say it enough," GD replied.

He's being really tender, Shonda thought, not knowing that his spirit already knew that his time was about to come to an end. Little did she know that GD was subconsciously bidding his farewells.

They had the deepest of conversations during that ride. GD was telling Shonda a lot of his childhood stories and most memorable times. He was also telling her about the times he was scared and times he wanted to give up on life when he was locked up, the feeling of betrayal by former friends and lovers. It was probably the most vulnerable side that he had shown her throughout their whole friendship.

"You know what scares me the most?" he asked.

"I didn't even know you even got scared until now," she replied.

"There was a time when I was around 19 and I got into it with this guy. The man pulled his tool to my face and threatened to blow my head off," GD started to share as Shonda listened in complete silence.

"I urged him on, but deep down I was scared shitless 'cause if he did pull the trigger, I didn't want to face Hell just yet. I begged God to spare me that day," he continued.

"I have done a lot of shit I can't take back, to the point I stopped confessing because I knew I would sin again." GD didn't blink. "Sometimes I wish I could take it back, I wish I didn't have to live this life, but I guess my fate was already predestined like Judas, except he had a greater purpose than me," GD let off a light chuckle.

They continued to drive until they started to see the city lights, and GD eventually got Shonda home and they talked until the sun came up.

"Don't forget about me, Shonda. I love you a lot, always remember that," GD said.

"Love you too. Why you saying it like that?" Shonda asked.

"Just wanted to say that," GD replied.

"Thank you for this gift, I'll always treasure it," she said before getting out of the car and walking to her door.

GD turned on his car and just before he pressed the gas, he saw Shonda go inside, as the door slowly closed and he continued to stare.

"Whatever happens, please be strong and continue your path," GD said and he drove off.

They would have several phone conversations up until two weeks before GD got murdered, but that day was the last time Shonda would see GD alive.

GD walked up to the building with his heart pacing. *Just go in and squash this,* he told himself as he waited for someone to open the front door. He couldn't sleep for the past four months and this was the moment he would end this ongoing beef. He just wanted to have this sit down and never see that face again. Enough is enough! He was going to be a bigger person and not resort to what he had always done.

Finally, a resident opened the front door and GD swiftly walked in. He would usually take the stairs, but something was prompting him to take the elevator. Something deep down was screaming at him to take the stairs but this sudden urge to wait for the elevator overcame his mind. The elevator doors opened, and he walked in, pressing the floor level. He waited for the elevator to reach its destination.

When the doors slowly opened, GD was greeted with objects piercing his chest. He barged out and ran towards the stairwell doors and ran flights of stairs. He felt excruciating pain throughout his body and the inner fire was burning him alive. He tried to remain calm so he wouldn't go into shock, but his asthma was flaring up from the intensity and he started to lose sight.

Bang Bang Bang!

GD found himself facedown on the cold concrete ground. His leg was hit, and he knew he wouldn't be able to get up in time. As he raised his head up, he barely saw the figure or figures hovering around him, mocking and laughing at their cold-hearted victory.

"Damn, homie, got caught lacking? Thought you were more smarter than that nigga."

"Go join your other niggas in hell, bitch ass!"

"You really think you ran the streets, my nigga? After what you did? Ha, it's a cold world, my nigga, just another nigga mommy got to bury."

GD try to speak, but instead blood filled up in his mouth.

"This nigga really want to have the last word. You been officially put in retirement, bitch. Time to go to bed."

Remember me, Shonda, please don't forget about me, please don't be mad, please don't get involved. GD thought of how Shonda would react when she found out what happened. He accepted his fate and used his remaining strength to form a huge grin.

The last thing GD saw was the Angel of Death waiting to take him home.

The day of the funeral was unbearable. Shonda didn't want to find closure and live in the fantasy that GD was still alive. But his boys kept knocking on the front door and rang her phone down until she complied. She sat in silence with cold-hearted eyes that sent shivers, and her heart was filled with boiling vengeance. His boys reminisced about GD's generosity and high school memories, while Shonda questioned why they let him die alone. Then she started to blame herself, about why she didn't nag him to tell her what was going on, that she should have called or hung out. She started to make a list of what ifs that could've prevented this. When she was offered a bottle of Clark's Court and Appleton, she didn't miss a beat on chugging them down and smoked a big spliff to her face. The sad thing about extreme grief is that no matter how high or drunk you try to get, it feels like you keep being sober.

They finally reached the church that GD grew up in and all she saw were undercover cars and visible police cars, and the leading investigators speaking with the family. She felt the numbness as she fought her legs to walk up the stairs, and once she opened the door she wanted to collapse as all the energies consumed the remaining joy out of her. GD's siblings motioned for her to sit at the front with the family by the pews, and one of them had to hold Shonda's arm to guide her. Shonda couldn't take her eyes off the open casket, a motionless person she once called friend. GD looked so different from the make up done by the morticians and bloated by the embalming fluids.

The service quickly began after Shonda made herself comfortable, which made her more enraged. The family brought up an old family friend who was rambling on and on about gun violence. He kept praising Jesus that his life was spared and went to details about how big the gun and wound he had. *Shut the fuck up,* she mumbled in her head, *yeah yeah Hallelujah, you alive but guess what bitch... MY FRIEND IS DEAD!* Shonda had to bite her tongue before it could disrupt the entire service. Then it was the family sharing, which had a mixture of laughter and mourning.

"He gave his soul to the devil, I watched him walk into his own demise and I couldn't help him," GD's grandpa fought his tears while surrounded by family. *I know he had faith,* Shonda told herself. *He acknowledges God, so he had to have some sort of salvation.*

After the Reverend shared his memories of GD when he used to go to Sunday school, he proceeded through hymns and prayers before it was almost time to close the casket. From the back, people came to pay their respects, and Shonda watched and observed all their faces. Some were well-known in different neighbourhoods and in the local music industry while others she questioned if they were foes.

When the Feds walked up, Shonda could have sworn she saw one of them sneer, which she wasn't surprised about because GD was known to fight them with their badges off and won. *Another grievance out your way eh*, she wanted to say out loud, but she held back; his family just wanted closure and the murderers locked behind bars, so she respected their wishes. *Let them do all the dirty work*, she smiled quickly but put back on her straight expression.

It was the family and close friends' turn, and Shonda stayed at the back while she endured the wailing and screaming from his loved ones. One of the aunts flung herself to the ground, while his mother continued to touch his neck and face as if she was trying to look for signs of life. Shonda walked up to the coffin and cupped his cold face with her hands. She was looking at him, but her mind wasn't there. GD looked like he was sleeping. *Wake up knucklehead*, Shonda repeated the phrase in her head. *I'm here silly butt, wake up!*

"Dwayne, please wake up... just open your eyes, you got me, okay." Shonda's eyes started to water. "Enough of this sick joke you trying to pull, you win, just please wake up... I miss you." A tear came down her eyes as she gently nudged him, in hopes he'll come back. But there was nothing.... His body seemed to grow colder by the second.

"I'll never forget about you," Shonda said in her most gentle voice. She kissed his forehead before returning back to her seat and she just stared.

When they tried to close the casket, that's when hell broke all loose with the endless screaming and shouting. His mother refused to let him go, and it took all of GD's siblings and friends to pull her back. She flung herself on the casket when it was closed. Some of GD's other friends put their heads down and had this chilling cry that Shonda would never forget. It took two of her boys to get Shonda on her feet and escort her to the car.

Shonda felt numb. She wanted to fling herself on the casket, she wanted to scream and punch the ground until her knuckles bled out. She wanted to go and spit at every "big man" in their face and call them cowards for not burying GD's murderers on the same day it happened. *If it wasn't for GD saving your asses, all of you would have been 6 feet deep and you can't get the bitchass!* she wanted to blurt out. She wanted to go up to the officers and give them a time limit before she went out and got street justice. She wanted to cry her heart out, but she couldn't; she continued to wipe her eyes and waited in the car.

When the funeral procession began, she felt like it was some kind of Godfather movie, cruisers from both sides lined up all the way to the burial grounds. Investigators were taking down license plates and taking photos of people. *Even in death you the talk of the town,* Shonda thought. They sang hymns when they lowered the casket while people had phones to record and threw flowers. His boys poured out large bottles of Henny and Appleton while Shonda silently said her prayers. It began pouring heavy and she wanted to stay, but she got cold and started coughing. Her boys held Shonda by the arms and took her back into the car. They drove back to the church so they could eat, but she wasn't hungry. She finally had some macaroni pie and cornbread when GD's mom gave her a plate.

"Please have something, sugarpie. He would hate to see you starve. He always told me you love food," GD's mom tried to cheer Shonda up.

Shonda gave her a faint smile and finished her plate before giving the family hugs and had one of his boys drop her home. That night she opened her drawer and took out the notebook GD gifted, and started to pour her heart out through ink and paper.

Shonda put on GD's necklace and it complemented her slender neck. She headed out to her show. She started her show with a dedication to GD and had other artists open up for her. She also had interactive activities during intermission and guest speakers on mental health.

Shonda performed her set and allowed some time for discussions, and it was a beautiful night. While people were heading out and her friends started to clean up, she snuck out and went to a corner to pour out all the Henny from a small bottle on to the pavement.

"This for you, GD," Shonda said out loud and looked up to the starlit sky and full moon. She closed her eyes and could feel his presence. Then she went back inside to help out.

That night when she finally got home, she crashed in her bed and fell into a deep slumber.

She found herself sitting on a beautiful wooden bench, watching the sunset by the water. This sunset was different, it was breathtaking, and the colours stood out much more than the other sunsets she had witnessed. It was something Shonda had never seen before, and she felt her body was so light that she could have sworn the wind could blow her away. She saw what looked like shooting stars going downwards into the vast ocean. All she felt was peace and joy surrounding her, every negative thought disappearing into the wind. Then an enormous full moon came out from the water, and the stars started to shoot upwards in all directions.

"Isn't it so beautiful, Shonda?"

Shonda jumped up at the voice and spun around to see GD wearing all red, from a fitted hat, hoodie and shoes, with diamond grills glistening in his mouth. She always knew he was rocking Bloodz but this was too much red, even for the likes of him.

"Dwayne, is that you?" Shonda cupped his face, and GD put his hand on top of hers.

"Thought you would never come, young lady," GD replied. "Come, let's sit down. I been wanting to talk to you."

He took her hand and they both sat down on the bench.

"I fucked up, Shonda. I probably still alive if I strapped up… but I wanted to do things differently," GD spoke in a low voice.

He turned to her and gave a big smile. "After our last conversation, I thought maybe I had a chance to make things right…. I guess that didn't go that well," he chuckled.

"But Shonda," GD put on a serious face, "you need to move on with your life. I already transitioned to the next, so you don't need to stress no more about the physical aspects of me."

GD held Shonda's face and had her facing him.

"Stay out of this fuckery, you hear me? This is not your war, and it wasn't even supposed to be mine, but I made it mine and look where it got me."

He stared so hard that Shonda could feel his entity pass through her like a winter's chill.

"You already remember me through your art, so don't stress yourself out over a piece of big stone."

GD's words startled Shonda for a bit. *But he's a spirit so he sees what's going on,* Shonda told herself.

"Plus, I like to remain hidden so I can have the element of surprise," he joked.

"I… I'm so sorry" Shonda started to tear up, and GD took out a red handkerchief and wiped her eyes.

"For what, silly? I got my judgment... ha...I guess prayers do come in handy, don't they. I got a chance to talk some sense into your head." GD had this beautiful bright smile, his face glowed like the sun disk.

In a far distance, a mighty angel and an enormous dragon walked across the water towards them. "All I saw was fire, Shonda... heard weeping and the gnashing of teeth," GD chuckled.

What on earth is going on, Shonda thought, then fear suddenly overwhelmed her.... *Did he see Hell?!*

"I told myself, 'This is it, Dwayne.' I thought I was going to be in torment for eternity... but I guess the angels

97

weren't going to let me go like that." GD pointed at the two entities moving closer to them.

At a near distance, the angel extended its huge hand, which looked like a football field in width, while the dragon extended its tail.

GD got up from the bench and Shonda followed right behind him.

"Shonda, remember what I said to you here… stay out of this and move on with your life." His words sent goosebumps all over Shonda's skin.

GD gave her one of his most beautiful smiles she had ever seen. "Wake up Shonda," he said tenderly. "You have to wake up."

"I don't want to, not yet," Shonda begged, but GD shook his head.

"Till we meet again." GD turned around and walked on top of the water towards the angel and dragon.

When Shonda tried to follow him, she fell underneath the water and when she felt her lungs filling with water, she woke up from her dream, gasping for air.

"Fuck!" Shonda exclaimed. She got up to wash off the sweat on her face and grabbed a glass of water before trying to dream of GD again. But it was just different dreams that had nothing to do with him, and she eventually woke up in the morning frustrated.

Shonda went to her drawer and grabbed the notebook and wrote in detail about the dream and felt the heaviness lift away. She got dressed and walked to her nearest florist and got a dozen white roses and a bottle of Henny before getting on the bus. After a few bus transfers, Shonda found herself in the same cemetery that caused her grievances years before. She walked to the same exact spot and poured some of the liquor before taking a shot, which made her cringe, so she poured out the rest. She placed the roses on the ground and said a prayer over the grave before looking at it for a few minutes in silence.

"Till we meet again my friend, till we meet again," Shonda said with a smile and as she turned around to go back home. She felt a warm presence and knew GD would be alright.

Blackout

Toronto Winter Power Outage 2013

"Oh great, here we go again! Arghh another blackout!" Diana exclaimed as she banged the computer table in frustration.

She had been working on her blog before all the lights went off. Annoyed, Diana pushed her chair in and made her way to the drawers, using her fingers to feel for any candles and her lighter. She lit the candles and placed them around the apartment. She felt her stomach rumbling and went to the kitchen to see what was there to eat. *Crap,* Diana realized she was so busy on her blog, she didn't get the chance to do her weekly grocery shopping. She went to bed hungry, hoping to sleep off her hunger until the lights came back on.

She didn't know how long she fell asleep for, but she was awoken by the door being unlocked. Diana got up and saw her partner Tyson at the door. She went up to him and they kissed each other before they both went to the bedroom. Both exhausted, they fell asleep in each other's arms.

Crash Crash Bang!

Later that night, Tyson and Diana jumped out of their sleep when they heard the loud noises. Tyson went to peek from their windows.

"Oh boy, they having a blast at Walmart!" Tyson laughed.

Diana raised her eyebrows and went to the window. Outside, across the street, were groups of people carrying electronics out of the store. She shook her head and was about to go back to bed, when they heard yelling and screaming in the hallway. She went out to the living room and stared at the door as she could hear a struggle ensuing outside. Tyson walked behind Diana and wrapped her in his arms.

"Baby, go to bed, it's none of our business," he urged her. She nodded and went to bed.

There were several occasions of shouting and loud sounds, but eventually they became used to it and fell asleep.

Diana's growling stomach woke her up and she went to wake Tyson up. It was still dark outside, and she was debating if it was worth the risk to go grab some snacks from the gas station.

"You want to eat, don't you?" Tyson mumbled as he rubbed his eyes.

Diana nodded as she rubbed her tummy and Tyson stretched his legs at the edge of the bed.

He walked up to turn the lights on, but after a couple flicks, he shook his head. "Damn, I think our building is out still," he exclaimed.

"Your phone got any juice left?" Diana asked.

Tyson went to the desk and turned on his phone.

"Yeah, got about 49 percent left since I put it on airplane mode," he answered.

Tyson turned on the flashlight from his phone to give the couple some light to change. He went to put on his sweater and a hoodie before putting his winter coat on. Diana put on several layers of sweaters before putting on her coat. Just when she turned the doorknob, Tyson put his hand on her shoulder.

"The hallway is going to be pitch dark, we need to be strategic," he advised.

"Don't they have emergency lights on in the hallway though?" she asked. *I mean, don't all apartments and condominiums have it?* she thought.

"Not in this hood," Tyson laughed to break the seriousness of this issue.

Talk about putting the safety of residents in consideration, Diana thought to herself, as she remembered other infamous housing complexes with flickering lights or pitch darkness. When she would go visit some of her friends, their families made sure she would come and leave before the sun came down or they would have her stay overnight.

"Here, take this." Tyson passed on a Nerf gun and a switchblade.

"Eummmm, is this the nerfed version of a pellet gun?" Diana nervously laughed. *What is this really going to do?* She had flashes of what ifs running through her head.

"I modified it. Just aim for the knees and balls," Tyson replied. He looked at her play with the switchblade cheerfully. "Ummm babe, you seem a bit too happy with it." He was beginning to wonder if it was a good idea.

"It's a beauty and plus it fits my hand so it's legal, haha," Diana said triumphantly.

"This woman." Tyson shook his head.

Once they stepped out and locked the door, Tyson had the flash on his phone and waved at the ground while Diana instinctively had her back against him, and they took each pace together. When they heard movements or their guts were saying something was wrong, he would use his hand to cover the light while Diana passed him the blade, while she had the Nerf gun ready to shoot. They slowly made their way downstairs, with the doors constantly opening and closing putting them on edge.

Once they opened the last door, Diana jumped and almost gun butted a youngster who was smoking.

"What the hell is wrong with your ol' lady, fam!! Wait... that's not even a BB..." The youngster stood amazed when he examined what Diana held.

"Sorry, just got spooked out." She was embarrassed for her reaction.

"It's all good... can't be caught lacking when there's a blackout," the youngster pointed out the chaos that was circulating.

The sun was slowly emerging, but with no lights on it was still very dark. But there was clear ice on the pavement outside and a hard ice crust on top of the snow resting on the grass. Every street and traffic light were frozen. There were branches frozen and shattered to pieces where they fell over. A big tree had ripped apart power lines and fallen onto a nearby street, blocking cars on either side. Other than it causing so much havoc in the city, it looked beautiful as the sun rays started to shine across the ice, making it look like a winter wonderland.

The outage would last for days, even weeks, in some parts of the city. Diana and Tyson found themselves stuck in the apartment for the majority of the time, only to go out when Tyson's homies would have goods for them to take back into the apartment. Every time they stepped out, it was as if they were in an urban labyrinth. Never knowing what could happen to them made their teamwork stronger, and the trust continued to be built. Diana was reading Norse mythology around that time and started to be paranoid about the Fimbulwinter as the days went by. Tyson would just be amused at how deep Diana was into the legends and started to read with her.

This blackout was a blessing in disguise, as the couple knew more about each other and their relationship was at its peak. It also showed how much a power outage can affect different communities, unraveling injustice and the lack of safety, which is negligence to one of the basic needs for people. What would be one's inconvenience could be another one's life or death.

The Gentile (Reject)

I stared at the cross in front of the sanctuary for half an hour now, talking to God about how tired I am of spilling my confessions, when I'll just commit the same sins once my footsteps out of His house. His Holy words lay across my hands, and I don't even know how I manage to hold the sacred book without being sent to hell.

"I don't see the point of coming back to You, if I would eventually turn my back against You again, O Lord," I cried out as I slouched my back against the pew. I put the Bible on my side and got on my knees with my hands out and wept from deep inside, that even the birds stopped chirping and the grasshoppers stopped singing. The slight breeze became still as I could sense the heavens open up with rays of light shining on top of my head. It felt warm, but cold in my stomach as if my head was a gateway to my yearning soul. But deep in my gut I took a dose of the harsh truth of reality: I would continue to allow the devil to win often, because our mortal shells are distorted, only until the final battle would God set me free.

Is it a curse that my fellow brothers and sisters could never accept me for my past deeds? I tried giving my best to be accepted since the day my grandma introduced me to her faith. Was I destined to receive half-hearted greetings, side glances and whispers in the sanctuary that was supposed to be a resting place from the outside world I constantly dealt with?

My grandmother's life was a true testimony of what Christ-like love meant; she knew exactly what I was doing, even if I did or did not tell her. I heard her prayers to God to protect me every morning before she started her day. Even after the restless nights I caused her, I would always be greeted back with unconditional love. I mention my grandmother's faith and love, because it'll be the only thing that I hold on to as I walk through the doors of any church, or through the valley of the shadow of death.

I had good and bad experiences in church growing up, but I always knew I was treated like an outcast because my lived experiences differ from those in the congregation. But I would still enjoy listening to stories from the Bible because they were relatable, and I grew particularly fond of King David, whom I am more open to have dialogue about in my future readings.

I finally got up from my knees and took a deep breath of air, allowing it to fill up every area of my lungs before letting it out through a big sigh. Running my fingers through the pages of the Holy Book, I stopped at the passage of Psalm 51 and read it aloud. Maybe there is a chance…. Just maybe if I hold on a bit longer.

"Bring your friends to our special Sunday service," a friend asked me in a lifegroup meeting on a Friday night.

"People already have an issue with my testimony, because of what I decided to be open with, and the friends I hung out with, and if they think I'm the spawn of Satan himself, then they really not going to like the others," I replied.

Those who know me for a while know how protective I can get with my friends, especially those who I know had faith but because of their lifestyle, churches shun them away. I refuse to put any of my friends in a space that would not accept them. And this broke my heart because I can feel their thirst for The Word and they do want to change, but don't know how to go about it.

There was a pastor who, when I started to go back to the community, I had no problems introducing all kinds of friends to. His heart is so big, and he had experience with similar hardships, but most importantly he was not afraid to be honest with us. He was the one who wanted to build connections with the neighbourhoods and meet them where they were at, other than the usual approach of getting people to enter the church to get support, etc. With his guidance and support from community leaders in a neighbourhood that was only a few blocks down the street from the church, we got to volunteer and participate in different events and it was genuine. Another thing I respected was his listening ears and open heart, something that is rare, because believers will start tuning out or rebuking "with love" once they hear a commandment being broken.

You spoke to me through The Ones known as "Gentiles"
Your Promise to the Land of Milk and Honey
Is most clearest
In forsaken territories.

You sent the most unlikely guardians
To pave the way...

I continue to go back and forth
As my heart continues to change.

My faith constantly went through hurdles, so much so that it became quite exhausting. It is true that to break bread among believers, in a gathering of two or more, the Spirit will be more present. But over the years I don't even bother myself to associate with any more communities. I am blessed enough to have two really close friends where I can still grow in faith together, and that is more than enough than to just keep running away.

They were of a different faith
But through them
I see The Truth
With clarity
For that
I pray that blessings continue to shower for the rest of
their days.

Some of my closest friends are of the Islamic faith, and we have always enjoyed sharing about our beliefs and learning from one another. In some of my darkest and loneliest times in my faith journey, they were the ones that reminded me of how powerful and healing faith can be. I found that I was able to listen to Him more clearly outside of the church rather than inside, because past hurts had made me cold. But when outsiders shared the same message, but in a different way, I was more in tune and softened my heart. I wanted to continue to thank them for being my support system, that we can have a healthy friendship through our similarities and differences.

Crawling under the cold sheets
Warming it up
With internal heat

Even in the dark
A tiny red book glowed.
My fingers traced through the words
Before drifting off to sleep.

I came to realize the path I chose
The faith I chose.

There will be no clear answer
Until I entered the era of the beyond.

If what was true
Or is true
There would be hope
For this Gentile soul

Trust Your Guts

Sandra blended her homemade hair food made out of avocado, egg, banana, coconut milk and some drops of vitamin E. She went to check her sleeping 8-month-old baby in the crib. *She'll be knocked out for another hour or so.* Sandra wanted to make use of every second of free time she had to self care. She poured out the contents into a bowl and parted her hair to put a slab into her scalp, using her comb to evenly distribute the mixture. After she was done, she wrapped it up and put her hair cap on and set her timer to 45 minutes. She went into the kitchen to start cooking lunch for the baby and her boyfriend. While she was wrapping up pork and chive wontons, she heard the door open and was greeted by her boyfriend, Paul.

"It'll be ready in about 15 minutes, love." Sandra kissed Paul on the lips.

"Where's Nisha?" Paul asked as he opened the fridge to grab the juice jug to pour into his cup.

"She's in the crib sleeping. I need to rinse my hair out," Sandra replied as her timer went off.

She finished cooking and put a bowl of hot wonton soup on a small dining table and went into the shower to wash her hair. The hot water felt so good running down her skin. She used the shampoo and worked the lather into the scalp and hair, then rinsed, and repeated this again to make sure no residue was left. She poured a generous amount of conditioner and put her hair up so she could focus on her body, cleaning her body with black soap. After she finished washing off everything, she went to dry her hair lightly and dried off her body. She put in some other hair products to further her hair treatment, before wrapping up her hair with a red silk wrap. She went into the room to put her red dragon kimono on.

"Thank you for the lunch, hunny... you look beautiful." Paul was behind her and kissed her neck.

"Baby, stop, I hear the baby crying," Sandra squirmed.

"Just wait until I get you all for myself." Paul gave her a seductive look.

"Yeah, well, not for a while, because everyone is going to be back from work." Sandra pulled on his pant strings. Paul bit his lips before going to comfort their child in the crib.

Sandra, Paul and their baby Nisha had been moving all over the Dundas West area, and finally moved in by St. Clair West with one of his uncles. It was a three-storey house and the couple were given the second biggest room in the house when Sandra got pregnant. There were other people that his uncle rented out to, and everyone played their part to contribute to the house – from collecting liquor bottles for some chump change, to other small hustles. Sandra saw them as her second family, and they all shared their food amongst each other.

There was one tenant in the house that everyone feared and loved. His name was Bonez. Bonez was barely home because he was constantly travelling, but he was the biggest breadwinner in the household. Whenever he came back, he would fill up the fridge for months, pay off the bills, and would give Paul a few rolls of money to help support Sandra and their baby. Everyone in the house knew what Bonez was doing but no one ever had a problem and did not speak.

It was almost 6, and Sandra made a big pot of shrimp scampi for dinner. Some folks came home from their day foraging and work and she served them their portions. After finishing off her plate, she started to wash the dishes.

"Hey babe, Nisha is being fussy again so I was thinking we should go for a walk." Paul came up behind Sandra.

"After I finish cleaning, I'll get ready," she replied before turning to kiss his cheek.

Half an hour later, Bonez opened the door and walked inside to greet everyone in the house.

"You good bro," Paul dabbed Bonez.

"Yeah, I'm blessed," Bonez answered and looked into the pot. "Mmmmm shrimp," he smiled as he served himself.

"Yeah, gotta thank you for buying that huge bag, though." Paul place a hand to his chest to show gratitude.

"No need to thank me, we family," Bonez replied as he made quick work of his plate.

Bonez let out a loud burp and rubbed his belly before sneaking something to Paul. "Can you do me a favour and hold this for me?" Bonez whispered in Paul's ear as he passed a brown paper bag.

"No worries, I got you, my nigga," Paul nodded as he slipped it under his hoodie. He walked into the bedroom and started to smile while shaking his head. "Saying you a Blood," he laughed.

Sandra changed out of her clothes and put on Paul's XXL red hoodie and black baggy pants, with a pair of all red and black sneakers that his cousin had gifted for her birthday. She had combed out her hair and straightened it, and she wore his red and black fitted hat.

"All the clothes are in the laundry and this all I could find," she shrugged.

"And explain Nisha's clothing." Paul raised his eyebrow and pointed at their baby.

Sandra had found a red onesie with the saying "I Got It From My Mama" and a pair of black pants with red baby shoes to put on the baby.

"It was to match." Sandra looked at Paul innocently.

"Uh huh." Paul kissed his teeth and got ready.

After he was dressed, they were all matching in red and black. When they walked out the door, they saw Bonez leaning against the side. He looked at them from head to toe and laughed.

"Look at the family of Bloodz," Bonez joked.

"Not you, too," Sandra gave him a cut eye.

"Don't shoot," Bonez laughed as he put his hands up.

"Very funny." She was not amused at all.

"Don't stay out too late though, this area is heated with them pork chops," Bonez caution as a police car passed by.

"We be good bro, just walk around the block until Nisha knocks out," Paul replied as he tucked the baby with a thick white blanket.

Bonez helped Paul take the stroller down and sent them off. It was quiet for the most part with the exception of sirens going off at a near distance.

"So much police around here," Sandra commented as she saw another 6 cruisers within a 10-minute span.

"Yeah I know," Paul mumbled under his breath.

They went around the block around three times and they were walking on their final round, when Sandra noticed the baby was fast asleep.

"The baby is asleep... we should start making our way back," she said as she fixed up the blanket.

"I want to take this other route I discovered the other day. It's nice and quiet and I know how much you love your nature walks." Paul directed Sandra to make a left instead of the right by the intersection.

Sandra didn't protest and was more than thrilled when she saw an entrance to a nearby forest. She could hear a loon and owls hooting while small brown bats flew around them. There was a bridge they crossed over, and saw a small stream making its journey under a dark tunnel. It probably took them about 45 minutes to finish the trail, but their home was around the corner. When Sandra was about to make a turn towards the house, Paul grabbed her and told her to go behind him.

"What's wrong, baby?" Sandra sounded concerned as she noticed Paul tense up.

"Something's not right…. Can you contact your mom to see if we can stay overnight?" he asked.

Sandra nodded and didn't ask any further questions and contacted her mom.

"Mom said we can stay for the weekend if you like," Sandra told Paul after she got off the phone.

"Yeah, we might have to stay longer because we might not have a place for a while," he replied.

"Huh, what is the matter?" Sandra asked.

Her question was answered in horror as she saw S.W.A.T. teams pinning down Bonez with an assault rifle and others tossed to the pavement in cuffs. Paul had to stop himself and hold Sandra back when they saw Paul's uncle being punched and kicked by an officer.

"Did you leave any IDs at the house?" Paul tried to remain calm and go through a mental list.

Sandra scrambled through her pockets and wallets and shook her head. Paul searched through his wallet and he was in the clear.

"I know a shortcut we can take so they won't see us." Paul pushed the stroller and took Sandra's hand.

"What about them?" Sandra tugged back, not wanting to leave the other people.

"Babes, we need to go or we all going to get time and lose our baby!" Paul pulled Sandra a bit harder.

Sandra fought her anger and eventually turned her back but cried once they were at a safe distance. They heard shouting and screaming from afar and the whole neighbourhood was peeking at the commotion. They hopped on the transit and travelled all the way to Sandra's mom's home. She put her emotions aside and put on an act so her family wouldn't worry. Her grandmother and mom were home and were ecstatic about seeing baby Nisha. Sandra's grandma made food and they fell asleep straight after dinner, because they were exhausted.

It was a couple of weeks that they had been sleeping over. One morning Paul got a phone call. He got the house keys and stepped out. Sandra woke up not too long after and went to check on the baby who was sleeping peacefully. Paul came back into the living room with a blank stare.

"Baby, are you okay?" Sandra asked as she walked up to him. "Baby, say something, you're scaring me!" She gently put her hands on his shoulders and gave him a light shake.

"They snitched on Bonez...." Paul slowly try to explain what he had heard.

"Snitched? Who?" Sandra pressed for more answers.

Neighbours? Can't be... they love him.... housemates? That doesn't make sense. Sandra's mind was racing.

"It's the other hustlers on the block that started talking to get rid of competition…. They also trying to get my uncle deported back to Guyana because he favoured Bonez over them," he sighed.

"The hell?!" Sandra was infuriated.

"They trying to pin everyone for this raid and if we came back any earlier, we would have been dragged into this," Paul said in a somber tone.

"That doesn't make sense…. How are you doing shit but want to rat?" Sandra scratched her head.

"Not everything is what it seems," Paul replied.

"So... what they find?" Sandra said quietly.

Paul whispered in her ear as he pulled out what Bonez had given and her jaws dropped.

"Damn, Bonez done for!" Sandra exclaimed.

"We are very lucky. We couldn't afford any of this for the sake of Nisha." Paul pulled Sandra closer and kissed her forehead.

Sandra went to the crib to cradle the baby in her arms.

"Always trust your instincts, baby girl…. Always believe your guts," Sandra whispered to their precious child.

Courthouse

The justice system and criminology had always fascinated me since I was a child. I would watch different shows that put their own spin on the court system, and how cases are being solved – to me, going to the libraries to read and talking to experts in their respective fields for facts and information dug deeper into my curiosity. There was one point in time when I wanted to get into forensic science and into the criminal justice sector so I could see whole stories unfold, but I wasn't too pleased with the lack of support for those who had potential and wanted to be integrated back into society.

I cared for the people that society deemed too much of an outcast to be part of a system that barely acknowledged them as humans. Though some crimes I found myself uncomfortable with, I believe that they shouldn't be refused basic human rights, as they are already paying for their crimes beyond their required punishment. But I would continue to learn more about the justice system on my own time and try to support my friends who were street-involved to the best of my ability, and to gain resources for them to use.

In high school, I quickly enrolled into the introduction of law class where we would visit the High Court to listen and study various cases, where we would apply the different lessons and hold discussions during recess and lunch break. My teacher would have our class follow some of the cases and I always found them intriguing. I grew quite interested in the different personalities of the people involved, and how it would make a big difference during hearings and sentencing. Though I ended up doing continuous co-op to graduate high school, my main focus was in the social work sector, so I wasn't too far off from my passion. For years, I was involved in different communities through the arts, assisting facilitators and also providing support for educators and city staff that wanted to support me in my goals.

Recently, I took up this program for a certificate that could get me into entry-level in the social work field, and a possibility to further my education. One thing I admired about this program was the fact that the majority of the staff had lived experiences as street-involved youth or had loved ones who were involved in the justice system. For the first time in an academic setting, I felt that I could be myself and be able to have heart-to-heart conversations about some past traumas I was coping with. Being able to move past some of them was a breath of fresh air.

In order to complete the program, I had to complete a few months of placement, and I was able to get into a program that provided support to youth that were in conflict with the law. Not to mention, the icing on the cake was that my supervisor pretty much jam-packed me with information and experience, from doing case management to going to courts for hearings and pre-trials and family visits. Though it was one of the shortest placements I had completed, the precious knowledge I received will forever be cherished. I want to thank my supervisor for pushing me out of my comfort zone (though I gave the "look"), and it motivated me to think outside the box and view scenarios from different angles.

I found myself being very invested in some of the hearings. Whether strangers or friends, there were things that got me on emotional roller coasters. *Why is that?* I found myself asking when tears built up for a family giving up their

119

eldest son, who was the breadwinner of the family. When I saw the families of the accused, and the families of the victim walking in, there was this dark aura that found itself seeping into my flesh and hitting the very core of my soul. When the children can't see their deceased parents anymore, or while watching the children of the other party watch their parents go in cuffs, my heart dropped. Some of the people I had never met or seen in my life, but yet my heart could feel their cries, and while I was tearing up, everyone in the room just had this blank stare.

In a field where you have to leave work at work and not take it home, I questioned myself every night for the past few months if I am even built for this. Only time can tell, it's a path I'm learning to not rush.

Prayers from different tongues can be heard throughout this place.
Families show the purest of love,
When it's time to give their loved ones away.

From the fairest of judges
Who gave out too many chances
The public shunned.
To the ones that will give the harshest of sentences,
They see no benefit
Other than behind bars.

I have heard screams after verdicts,
Dreaded sounds of cuffs on our young.

Clench in silence
Grinding teeth,
Innocent pleading guilty

While monsters walk free
With a grin to mock.

Victim statements can stir rainstorms,
Regretful looks from accused
Can melt people's hearts.

A merry-go-round of emotions,
You'll laugh
Cry
Be angry
All at the same trial.

Escape from the Jungle

"What are you up to tonight?" Gladys asked on the phone.

"I'm going to the west," Alicia responded.

"Who you meeting with?" Gladys asked.

. "This guy I've been talking to, I'm going to his place," Alicia answered.

"I'm coming with you," Gladys quickly replied. No way in hell was she allowing Alicia to go to this man's house on her own.

"Really... I guess you can come but dress up please," Alicia pleaded.

"You already know I'm going to dress comfortably." Gladys rolled her eyes.

"Oh fine, meet me at Downsview Station," Alicia said.

Gladys hung up and got dressed. She got to the subway station and waited for Alicia to come.

"Girl, you look like a fucking goon!" Alicia face palmed while looking up and down at Gladys black puffer jacket with an oversized dark blue jersey, a black Blue Jays fitted hat with her red streaked hair out and black baggy pants. "Now what am I going to tell this dude about you?!"

"That's none his concern with his dusty ol' ass," Gladys sneered.

"Ugh, I swear I can't take you anywhere," Alicia said in frustration.

The girls took the subway down to their designated station and hopped on a bus to get to their destination.

"He said he got a friend to keep you company," Alicia said after she checked her BBM (Blackberry Messenger).

"Oh, that's so considerate of him," Gladys replied sarcastically.

They walked towards a house and saw a tall medium-built man with black hoodie sitting on the porch. The guy walked up to them to hug Alicia and kiss her forehead. He then looked at Gladys and gave her a weird look before straightening his face and extending his hand.

"Let me introduce myself. I go by Carlos," the man said as Gladys shook his hand. He had a full set of diamond grills and the streetlights were showcasing the cuts and quality of the precious stones.

"Damn, your mouth is blinding me," Gladys squinted her eyes and Carlos laughed.

"Come inside." Carlos opened the door for the girls.

Gladys grabbed Alicia's hands and spun her around to face each other.

"What the fuck are you thinking, we don't even know this nigga." Gladys was tightening her grip.

Alicia giggled and wiggled her hands out of Gladys' grip and just shrugged.

"It's cold outside, let's just go," Alicia said, frolicking in.

Gladys body tensed up, but she followed her friend instead, and they ended up sitting by a table in the living room. Carlos tried to offer the girls some drinks and smokes, which Alicia happily accepted. Gladys declined and just tried to think of other things to pass the time. Her stomach suddenly started churning, and when she turned her head to look at the stairs leading from the basement, she saw three men walking upstairs.

Gladys glared at Alicia and then at Carlos. "So, what happened to only you and your friend?" she asked in a tense voice.

Carlos didn't answer as the other guys hovered around them in the living room. Gladys reached into her pocket and wrapped her fingers around an object, which provided her some sense of security. The group of men looked around mid-twenties except for one man with a certain aura. The older man must have been around 6 foot 5, had dreads down to his waist, and was muscular with both arms covered in tattoos and scars, with a bottom set of gold grills. For some reason Gladys felt alright with him. *He's definitely the OG and has sense unlike these assholes,* Gladys thought to herself.

"This my road dog Unks," Carlos introduced the older man to Gladys and Alicia. "This my cuzzo Smokey." He pointed to another man who was short and stocky, with a dark red beanie hat that hovered just above his eyes. Gladys had a bad feeling with him and wanted him to leave.

"You can call me Ruckus," a man with wiry physique said while sitting down across the table. He wore designer glasses, which made his eyes look more alluring, an enormous gold cross necklace, and a silver brass knuckle on his right hand.

"Why you ladies so tense," Unks read the girls body language on the spot.

"Oh, I don't know…" Alicia replied in a sarcastic voice while being animate with her hand motions. "Maybe because I was told I would be with Carlos, and there'll be a friend for my homegirl here!"

Unks gave a look of disapproval towards Carlos and pulled Smokey aside. "Yo, what did I tell you about pulling this type of stunt, young nigga," Unks whispered to Smokey.

"They just cyatties, Unks… easy kill," Smokey grinned.

"If you don't stop thinking with your dick, and not with your head you'll end up in a body bag, son," Unks said through his teeth. He shook his head and they went back into the living room. "I'm going to head to the basement," he told everyone as he walked downstairs.

"Same here," Ruckus joined Unks with Smokey, following him close behind.

Carlos excused himself from the girls to talk to Smokey for a moment. Gladys started to fidget with her phone and looked at Alicia. Alicia was becoming turnt, but she was still aware of her surroundings, and was beginning to change her mind. She typed into her BBM and showed Gladys – *Let's cut*. Gladys nodded and was about to leave, when they saw Smokey around the corner leaning against the door. Alicia and Gladys looked at each other in shock.

How did they not hear any sounds when they were at the living room?

"Buses stopped running already, and I don't want you ladies to be walking so far this late. Just chill here until it's 6," Smokey said in a sly tone.

"We good," Gladys sounded agitated.

"C'mon, stop being so tight up," Smokey replied.

"Only till 6. buddy," Alicia nudged at Gladys' arm.

"Yes of course," Smokey walked ahead of them and they followed suit.

When they turned the corner, Gladys stopped and stared at the basement. There were five other boys no older than their late teens lying on the couch with their phones and playing video games. Alicia didn't budge when Carlos tried to take her hand. Gladys pointed at the sofa that was furthest away from the men, and they both sat down. Smokey was introducing the others, but Gladys and Alicia couldn't care less who they were.

Unks kept walking in and out of the basement after picking up calls, but he kept checking in on how the girls were doing. Smokey tried to offer them shrooms and other pills, which Gladys kept declining. Alicia was starting to catch an attitude with Smokey, but Carlos kept talking to her. Unks came back again with a Gran Patron Platinum bottle and tried to offer it to the girls. Alicia only accepted the offer, because Unks believed that women should always get an untouched bottle and pour their own. Gladys could barely stand the scent and shooed it away when Alicia tried to pass her a glass.

126

"So why you dressing up like me? I'm starting to think you pull 24/7 shifts like me," Unks asked Gladys.

"Am I not allowed to be myself and be comfortable in what I wear?" Gladys shot back.

"Well, you're right" Unks shrugged and looked at his phone, "I'm gone till later... now make sure y'all behave." He bowed to the ladies and left.

Not even a few minutes later, Smokey and Ruckus started to bring up sexual fantasies and past sexual experiences. Alicia just looked on her phone and played games while Gladys played "God of War III" and "Bayonetta" with Carlos, both attempting to tune out the discomfort of the conversations.

"So... you girls ever heard of running a train?" Ruckus asked.

"The fuck?!" Alicia put her phone down.

"Repeat yourself... again!" Gladys changed her tone of voice and slipped her blade into her sleeve for easy access if it was necessary.

"Relax! It's was just a simple question," Smokey jumped in. "Guess y'all never been around niggas before," he snickered.

"No no, I just haven't been around sex-deprived predators that often, so I do apologize," Gladys answered calmly.

"You're a feisty little kitten, aren't you," Smokey responded, appalled.

"I'm glad you know... me-motherfucking-ow," Gladys clawed the air.

Smokey changed topics, but it already left a negative wedge between them. Time passed and Gladys' eyelids began to feel heavy, but Alicia kept trying to whisper and shake Gladys' arm, to no avail. The last thing that Gladys remembered was seeing Ruckus snoring, before she ended up falling asleep.

"Gladys, wake up! It's 6 now... let's dip." Alicia nudged Gladys who woke up and wiped away her drool.

Only Carlos and Smokey were still awake, and Alicia must have been conversing to keep an eye on them. Alicia put on her jacket while Gladys yawned and she got up, forgetting about her prized possession in her sleeve. In slow motion, Alicia watched as Gladys' protection slipped out of her clothing.

The room went dead silent after the blade made contact with the floor. It felt like hours when it was merely 5 seconds, but Gladys didn't know if she would see past this crucial moment. The men glared at the Nubian beauty with curves made perfect to slice effortlessly. Gladys saw confusion mixed with fear in their eyes and made full use of her advantage in the situation. She grabbed the blade. and used her black bandana she had in her pocket to wipe the dirt off. Gladys started to do some tricks with the sharp eye empress to display its full potency.

"You gwan like a bad gyal eh," Carlos made his remark.

"Just because I'm a girl, does it mean I can't defend myself? Mark... my... words... I bite just as hard as I bark," Gladys hissed and snapped her teeth, while placing the blade back into her pocket.

"Oh! And one more thing... or should I say advice, for future purposes... I live by this motto, 'You don't know who I am or who I know and I don't who you know'... so, let's keep this cordial and have a nice day, gentlemen." Gladys glared at Smokey dead straight in his eyes, and had Alicia walk up the stairs first.

While putting on their shoes, Gladys could hear Carlos and Smokey talk about what had happened. Smokey was also yelling at Carlos about bringing crazy women to his crib, and she couldn't help but give off a light chuckle. She despised people who always tried to prey on fresh meat, but also thankful that nothing more serious occurred behind those jungle walls. Alicia and Gladys got outside the house and walked past the big mall to reach the bus stop on the other side. Even when Carlos called out for them to come back to make amends, the girls didn't look back and hopped on the bus.

Never again to return to the heart of the jungle...

Drainage

"Hey guys I'm here... have to turn off my phone," Mariah sighed as she stood in front of the building.

"Make sure you call us back when you done, girl. We love you," one of her friends said in the joint phone conversation.

"Love you guys too," Mariah replied and turned off the phone.

She opened the door and forced herself up the stairs, with each step getting heavier than before. By the time she had three more steps to go, she had to literally drag her feet while fighting herself to turn back around and run. She finally found herself in front of a door and pressed the buzzer.

"Good morning miss, how may I help you?" A man's voice spoke through the speaker.

"I have an appointment for this morning at 8:30," Mariah replied in a soft voice.

She heard papers rustling for a few seconds and then there was a moment of silence.

"Please come in," the man said, and Mariah heard the door unlocked.

Mariah took off her coat, hung it on the coat rack, and proceeded to go through the reception. After a few minutes and answering a few questions, the guard unlocked another set of doors for Mariah to come in through. The guard checked her phone and gave her a strict warning about keeping it off, or face being banned. She nodded and walked towards the end of the waiting room and sat down. She looked around and only saw one elderly man going through some magazines.

As minutes passed, Mariah's anxiety increased, and she started to debate with herself – to stay or leave. *What the hell am I even doing here,* she started to ponder. *I'm going to get back at him.* She started to become angry as she replayed the conversations she had with her friends and the one who impregnated her. *I should have known, but I was still bleeding,* Mariah blamed herself for allowing this to go so far.

"Oh, why you waited so long," he said as he stared into her soul.

"I was still bleeding… you make it sound like I want this… I didn't know!" She cried out as she fought the urge not to slit his throat and spit at his face, while she envisioned him choking on his own blood.

"Liar! You knew what you were doing all along!!" He continued his heartless trend.

"If I did, I wouldn't have fucking told you, asshole!" She almost screamed but didn't want to wake anyone in the household. *"You think I'm like your other bitches that want to trap you my nigga?!! I don't need you for shit!!!"*

He was
Cold hearted
&
Heartless!
But what is there to expect?

131

If the trenches choked his soul
So his heart
Would
Hurt
Less!

But maybe a little hurt
Would be better than blank eyes...

Maybe a hug
Or
Walk through a park...

Would show the love
He often spoke of,
While holding me close into his arms.

Death chamber more scary
When you have to do it alone.

The dead haunts more
When there is no one to take me home.

He's going to regret this. Mariah could feel her chest burning in hatred from the memories.

Thankfully today was not as busy as the day before, she thought as she recalled how packed it was when she walked in. There were tons of men of all ages in the waiting room, and she noticed that men of all other races other than her own were accompanying the women. When she saw her people the women either came by themselves or the men dropped them off and left, didn't even return after the women were finished. This made Mariah more infuriated

132

and some of the men noticed her silent anger, because they started to feel uneasy around her.

"Pieces of dog shit," Mariah mumbled as she cracked her knuckles to avoid punching through the walls. Her legs started to shake, so she used her elbows to pin them down and covered her face with her hands.

Breathe in and out, she told herself as she tried to relax her body. *You been drinking and smoking this whole time.* She kept coming up with reasons to hide the fact that she didn't want to go through with this.

"Mariah? Mariah Thompson?" A woman's voice called out from an opaque glass office.

"Here I am," Mariah answered as she got up from her seat and brushed off the dust from her grey joggers.

She walked inside the office and gently closed the door. The woman's voice belonged to this beautiful young lady who looked like a nursing student and was in a casual blue shirt and black jeans.

"Do you have your health card with you?" The lady smiled at Mariah.

Mariah reach for her wallet to pull out her health card and put it on the table before she sat down.

"Thank you," the lady said as she reached for the card and started to write in lightning speed through the paperwork.

After the lady was done, she had Mariah to put her signature and initials on the lines with an X.

Mariah skimmed through the paragraphs to avoid looking at the questions that would trigger her, but the last question had her bite the inside of her cheeks.

"On the scale of 1-10 how sure are you with going through with this procedure?" the question asked, with 10 as the most confident. Mariah stared at the question for some time, which made the lady look at her.

"Is everything alright, Miss?" The lady asked in a concerned voice.

"Yeah... everything is alright," Mariah lied as she circled 10 to the question and returned the paper.

"Good," the lady smiled as she stamped the papers and put on a medical wristband on Mariah's left wrist. "Follow me," the lady instructed her as they both got up and went through another set of doors. The lady showed Mariah her change room and locker and gave her further instructions. Mariah took everything off below her waist and kept her socks on, put on a gown and went to sit at a smaller waiting room. She sat in the room and she found that it was much cooler than the other rooms. She wrapped herself up with a blanket provided to her and waited.

"I'm really sorry... I'm really sorry," Mariah spoke softly to her stomach while rubbing it in circular motion. "I failed as a mother... I'm weak and you don't deserve it," she continued to speak as she waited for everything to be over and done with.

A nurse came to fetch her to get her bloodwork and ultrasound done. While getting the procedure done, the nurse must have forgotten to turn the screen away, because

Mariah fully saw everyone on the screen. She quickly turned away to rub a tear trickling down and continued to wait for the nurse to finish the routine.

After she was finished the nurse took her into a small room and told her lay down on the medical table, and once the doctor came in. Mariah knew this was the point of no return.

Her holy temple was being invaded.
She groaned as she felt
Every...
Inch...
Of sacredness
Go through the drainage.

Pride is what kept her intact...

Her eyes wandered as she saw the screen of death,
Wrapped around life
To dismiss its existence
With one suction
Wall scratching
At a time.

Innocence disappearing,
Future plans
&
Dreams cease to exist

It was finally over and Mariah was escorted into the recovery room. She felt empty and a sudden wave of loneliness covered her like an eerie veil. She continued her act of being cheery and even joked with the other patients and nurses.

A book on the small wooden block beside her caught her eye. She picked up the book and saw that it was a therapeutic colouring book. *Ooo that's pretty neat,* she thought as she was trying to distract herself. She flipped through the pages and saw different pictures that the women before her started to colour and she saw poetry and reflections on the blank pages. She started to colour in the blank spots and finished some drawings, while writing notes of love into the book. The words she wrote in that book was all the remaining tenderness she had left in her. The nurse came to do a final check up on her and provided antibiotics.

"I booked you in two weeks for your check up, Miss," the nurse told her while giving Mariah an appointment card.

Mariah turned her phone back on and saw unread messages from the man she had once cared for.

She was about to open the messages, until she felt the emptiness of her womb hover above her. She felt a ghostly figure circling around her, before a small cold hand brushed her fingertips. Mariah jumped before speed walking towards the bus stop.

"I love you, Mommy," a childlike voice whispered into Mariah's left ear.

Mariah felt an ice-cold kiss on her forehead, and it made her scream, causing some pedestrians across the street to stare at her. She quickly ran after the bus and got back home feeling drained.

That night she tossed and turned in her bed, before getting up to pour herself a glass of milk. She swore she heard little footsteps but didn't pay no mind to them since she was exhausted. *Must be hallucinating,* she reassured herself and chugged down the milk and washed her cup.

"I love you, Mommy," the same childlike voice whispered, but Mariah couldn't tell where it was coming from.

"Okay... I need to stop watching ghost documentaries," she told herself as she raced to get under her blanket.

Just when she got to her room and put her hand to turn the doorknob, she noticed a huge moth on the bathroom door from across the hallway. Mariah continued to stare at the moth before taking a couple steps towards it. She ran back into the room when the moth suddenly flew towards her. She put her bed covers over her head and tried not to spook herself out anymore.

"I love you, Mommy.... I'll always love Mommy." The voice continued throughout the night.

My womb is empty
But I can still feel ghostly kicks.

Hearing tiny voices pleading
Sleep became a nightmarish dungeon
I can't seem to wake up.

A couple of weeks after, Mariah was asked to perform a spoken word piece and run a workshop for groups of high school girls. The last group she was teaching was a bit rowdy at first and some of the girls were even giving her attitude. But they all became attentive and calmer when Mariah read her piece of her recent ordeal. After her program wrapped up, she was cleaning and felt a light tap on her shoulder. She turned around and faced a young girl with watery eyes who was also constantly rubbing her stomach.

"So, you have some time or you in a hurry?" the young girl asked in a timid voice.

"I have no plans after this. What's on your mind?" Mariah asked.

"I… took in your poem and felt deeply connected to it…. Do you mind sharing with me about the backstory of your piece?" the girl quietly asked.

The teacher nodded her head of approval and put her hand up to indicate they have ten minutes left. Mariah and the girl walked to a nearby bench facing a small pond and had the most necessary healing conversation she had in years.

"I feel weak… I failed as a mother…" the girl said in a soft voice. Mariah barely heard her with the wind whistling its song.

"You'll be alright… we'll be alright together," Mariah encouraged the girl while convincing herself.

"I never got your name," Mariah asked.

"My name is Gloria… Gloria O'koye," the girl answered.

"You are very strong, Gloria…. When you are ready, just remember that your art will save lives," Mariah told her.

"My art will save lives… my art… will save lives…" Gloria repeated the phrase as she started to make her way back to her classmates.

Mariah took a deep breath before making her way back home, and said, "Believe in yourself just like how I believe in you."

Hood Chronicles Song List - Part II

Cdet aka Mr.G - Unthinkable/I'm Ready Freestyle
Lyfe Jennings - Made Up My Mind
Huncho Prime - Only The Family
DMX Feat. Faith Evans - I Miss You
Huncho Prim e- Seen The Most
GhostFace Killah Feat. Mary J Blige - All I Got Is You
Txnic Feat. Jamie Kingpin x Mack10 - Nah Foreal
Tupac - They Don't Give A Fuck About Us
Golde London - MOBB
Tracey Kayy - Memories
Lola Bunz - West End
Shortiie Raw - My Crown
Boosie Badazz Feat. Lyfe Jennings - Cold Hearted
Twista Feat. Faith Evans - Hope
Blacus Ninjah - Thinking About You
Casey K Jonesz - Spooky Snoopn
Dreams Brown Feat. Alicia Cinnamon - Fall To Rise
Kanye West - Thru The Wire
Ash Kardash - In My Feelings
Golde London - Callin Me
Kaptaiin - Switch
Serani - Stinkin Rich
Csin - Exhale
Nathan Baya - This Far
Heartless G. - Gangsta Movie
Lil Wayne - I Miss My Dawgs
Trey Songz - Gotta Make It

Boosie Badazz - So You Wanna Be A Gangsta
Geezy Loc - Ride With Mine
Tanya Stephens - These Streets
Boosie Badazz Feat. Webbie - Smoking On Purple
Lyfe Jennings - Cry
T.I. -You Ain't Missing Nothing
Jah Cure - Prison Walls
Sling Dadz - I'm From Jane
Nathan Baya - Freedom
Ammo - Suicidal Man
Baadass Bukk x Lola Bunz - Stay Schemin Remix
Lola Bunz x Rushiie Raw x Baadass Bukk x Rootz - Jane
    and Finch Female Cypher
Corey Fila Feat. C4 x Papa Corleone - Im From The Finch
Lyfe Jennings - Must Be Nice
Golde London - In My Own Zone
Heartless G. - It's On
Baadass Bukk - Army Of Angels
Boosie Badazz - Hope I Make It
Raz Fresco - 92 Ski Lo
Heavy Steve Feat. Tanisha - One Heavy Dream
Boosie Badazz - Granny Granny
Lyfe Jennings - 26 Years 17 Days
Jadakiss - Things I've Been Through
Ammo - Deeper Aspects
Boosie Badazz - Hospital
TMC McCrea - Holy Ghost
NessGotem x Papa Corleone - Cards Given
Webbie - If I Was A Fifth
Wale - Family Affair
PolloMadeIt - Get Right
T.I. - I Still Love You
P. Reign - Angels
Trick Daddy Feat. Latcha Scott - Thug Holiday
Lil Wayne - I Miss My Dawgs

You Know You In The Hood When...

When Elevators Have Their Own Schedule

↳ Here's a piece of advice: take the stairs if possible, and always remember to AVOID TOUCHING THE RAIL!!!

When It's The Holidays: Take Heed

When It's The Holidays: It Is Or Is It Not

When It's The Holidays: Locals Know Best

Extreme Sports On The Block: When They Take Bike Riding To A Whole New Level

Extreme Sports On The Block: And Skipping Rope

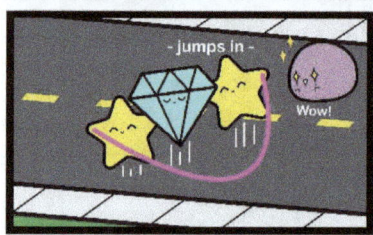 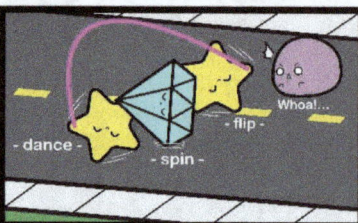

Extreme Sports On The Block: Don't Forget Those Hula Hoops

Didn't I See This Before?

When You Play "Hot Or Cold"

Cornered

White Lie

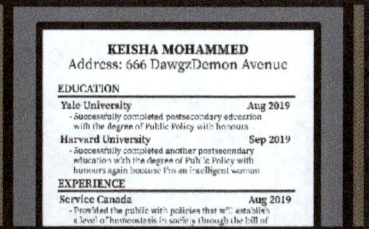

Who Needs A Wallet When...

Different Folds Of Money

From The Heart

Beyond

When Nipsey Hussle passed away, I started seeing my newsfeed and stories flood with his music, interviews and quotes. It went on for about a good two weeks, then it gradually calmed down. I do still see a couple of posts of wisdom about him here and there, yet it eventually becomes rare until his birthday and death anniversaries come up… just like how it usually goes. I do hope there'll be a movement that will not disintegrate, a last wish that won't be forgotten. When someone famous or close to my heart passes on, it puts me into a meditative and reflective state. I start to question about letting those who are important to me know how much I really appreciate and cherish them. I question about telling them how they are always dear to my heart. I find myself showering love and encouraging phone calls and texts to family and friends. When I share with them how much I love them, they brush it off or laugh because they not use to me being open.

I am reminded of the last day I spoke to my grandma, when I told her I love and miss her, she just told me I know and let it at that. She never told me I love you back and just said don't mention it because it's affecting her pulse. It really hurt me, but I know she didn't want to get emotional. That was probably the only time I ever told her upfront I loved her. Treating each moment as my last, it bothers me that it takes tragedies for that harsh reminder that there is no guarantee. Yet grief has become this addiction that has spread in societies like wildfire.

"Buried 6 feet deep seems to
Bring family together,
Friends disappear,
Haters praise your name

With the same tongue that once cursed you like no tomorrow"

At times we wait till the last moments or when it's too late to make amends. We often throw a bigger gathering for the celebration of life, breathtaking speech for the eulogy, and countless stories that make strangers want to know the person. Maybe it's pride, grudges or fear of the unknown that stops us. Perhaps we feel that our love goes better unheard, in silence till they are in eternal rest.

We celebrate the dead more than we celebrate the living
But who am I to judge,
When I tell her grave "I love you" and "I miss you" more
Than when she was still breathing.

I'll surpass visiting her tomb more than when she was alive
Yet she says she'll be a distant memory
Cause she's at peace
While I have to continue to put up a fight.

"Don't have to worry for a departing spirit like me, Sze-Ming"
The last day she spoke.
"Visit me once in a while"
"Make sure you take care of your mother and daughters"
"My physical body will eventually be no more"
"It shall return back into dust"

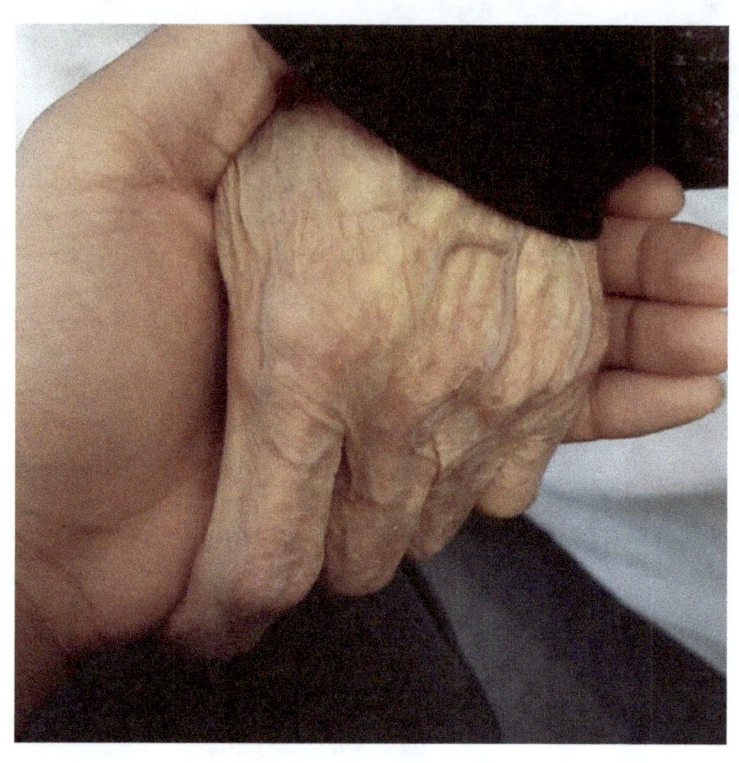

However
I attend to her resting place religiously.
Dedicated to gifting her White Lilies and Gladioli
Than offerings for the church she raised me in.

Two years pass
They say time will ease the pain.
I believe
I have faith

Even though my homies come see me during nights
I wipe my tears
So my children will see that their mother will be okay.

154

Some of my loved ones that are in conflict with the law or growing up in at-risk neighbourhoods were close to their elders. I would hear stories of laughter from reminiscing, and at times it got emotional to the point that tears would be fought back. Grandparents played a huge role in my friends' lives and in some cases, one of their biggest regrets was causing their grandparents so much grievances, even though all they received is love from them. I would have heart-to-heart moments with the ones who are locked up when receiving news that their grandparents passed on, and they couldn't make it to the burial grounds till they finish their sentences.

Some of my loved ones started to lash out after their grandparents' passing. They were honour roll students, on the road to achieving good careers, a path full of success and joy when their elders were still alive.

Like lanterns that light up the night sky
Complement the moon during Mid-Autumn Festival

They were like prized harvest within the family trees
Passing down traits from the sturdiest of roots
Not even the strongest gusts of wind could've overtook.

I witness individuals with hearts of gold
Turn to hearts of crumbling stones.
I witness my own destruction....

I'd painfully watch the ones that I once looked up to become a totally different person.

Clarke's Court
Smoking on Purple
Can never numb the pain away

Embracing funerals after yours
Was a way my mind could falsely escape.

A human life became garbage
A human life taken cannot affect their soul.
Had they transformed into a heartless beast
Or a persona to get away from the original cause.

After burying my grandmother, I became hostile and instigated arguments to lash off my grief. What kept me out of a dangerous spiral was the welfare of my children and the fear of being incarcerated from the unknown extent I'll go for in my emotional state. Humans underestimate how vulnerable and clouded your judgement gets when going through grief. Also, I was affected by the experience of losing friends behind bars because of this very reason. I was fortunate to have thought things through. This topic is something I prefer having an in-person dialogue about; can't find words to describe my thoughts in this book.

However, I want to end the part with this:

"I wish that society can learn how to appreciate the ones here, instead of worshipping those who already transitioned to the next. Their task and journey in this world have been completed. It's time for us to continue our adventure to the fullest, to fulfill our adventure."
– Glowz

In Memory of Wai-Ming Lee
December 21st, 1924–May 11th, 2017

Dear Black Man

Dear black man,
you showed that complete devotion equals to heartbreaks
and tears.
You taught me that no matter how much I invest in you
With time
Money
And Actions....
I would be the cold-hearted witch as we part ways
when your cup has finally overflowed.

Dear black man,
I learn to demolish any feelings after a few weeks
So my walls can repair itself
Once I sense it has started to display cracks.
I learn to become selfish and keep my
Wealth to myself and lie that there is nothing to give.

Dear black man,
I still want to love you
Even when the Nile that keeps me alive has become
poison with your flaws.

*I would still speak out and cover my body over yours as
bullets decorate my back for practice*
as you cry out to spare your life after disposing mine.

I had aborted bloodlines at your command
Yet will still birth nations to continue your lineage.

Dear black man,
I would never allow outsiders to put you down
Even after you deem me as worthless
Cause my love is unconditional for my black men.

158

I guess I'm under the influence of chocolate high.

Dear black man
I crave and seek for you
Like an orphan praying for their parents to resurrect.
What was impossible to stop a generational curse.

Dear black man
<u>I still love you</u>
<u>And always will love you.</u>
Stop shattering my reflection and then call me broken

Music to My Ears, Mind & Soul

Music is everything to me. Through music, stories and words are shared, giving listeners the voices of people's hearts. There is always at least one catalogue of music that a person can relate to, be triggered by, or be soothed by, to any emotion or situation. Music is the therapy that can reach into the cracks of the internal walls in any walk of life. Throughout my childhood, I was exposed to different genres of music; it brought communities together, families together, and much more.

I don't mind listening to party music and that bump-your-head kind of music, but it was that soul music, that story-telling music that you knew it came from a deep part of the heart, that sucked me in. I replayed the songs until I memorized them and could visualize the words without watching the music videos. It hit deeper when the song described a situation word-for-word, as each detail dug up pent up emotions. There were songs that I have been listening to ever since I was a child, but the lyrics struck me hard when I was going through similar scenarios; songs like "What's Going On" by Remy Ma featuring Keyshia Cole, "Granny Granny" by Boosie Badazz, "Just For A Moment" by Nas featuring Quan, etc.

I was a hermit for a few years, and continued to play songs in my music vault, so when I started to get back into the world, I noticed lots of the messages in music have changed. Some of the styles I found it a bit hard to tell the artists apart, and I found myself being pretty close-minded to exploring new music to add in my personal collection. Mainstream music barely had a place in my heart anymore, unless someone recommended it to me, or if I listened to a catchy tune that was replayed almost a million times on the radio. Sometimes I would just find the instrumentals of these songs and write my stories and poetry to them, yet I even preferred the parody versions over the actual songs. To be very honest, some of these songs I wouldn't mind if they were played years before, when artists had their own flow and individuality.

However, it also challenged me to explore more into local artists to find the hidden gems. I had always been listening to underground music, but this time around, I had the courage to go out to events and share with the artists how impactful their art was. It's amazing how much talent is within our radar, yet we tend to give more attention and respect to outsiders. This is pretty normal, but when I travel to other cities, plenty of people would always put their own artists first and the outsider had to put in work to earn that love.

These days I would take my time scrolling through artists' pages and listening to their upcoming music. I do take in that some artists are very big on the street life. The theme is fine with me, because I do love my hood music (especially when I bump some Palm Beach County tunes) – I can get pretty rowdy. Yet when I take in some of the content in the lyrics, there is this pause in my brain before I ask myself, *Why?* I do find that some of the audience only absorb the surface content and want to be involved without knowing all the side effects of the lifestyle. Mind you, the trend has been going on for years, but these days… it feels like it has gotten worse…. Or maybe I'm just acting like my parents when I was bumping to 50 Cent's "Power Of A Dollar."

My fellow artists, please take heed, for a peaceful and smooth journey to the artistic world, there is a limit to how open and involved into hood politics you can be. You are restraining yourself from future opportunities. There is no issue with exploring other concepts, even if your audience may question your authenticity, as it is your own story, and in life there is growth, because to remain in one mindset will only put a halt to your dreams. Don't cause yourself to stumble because of fear; do not be afraid to change your environment. Your chapters have already been set in stone, and your true fans will encourage you to mature as an artist and as a person.

Music has a powerful influence on society, whether you believe it or not. We have seen from time to time how music has been a major trendsetter. Music is one of the key gateways into building connections and sparking up conversations; it also reveals the health of the society even though censorship tries to sugar-coat it.

Music holds a special place in my self-care toolkit, one of the most therapeutic ways to cheer me up on a down day. It is as powerful as spending time with nature when used properly. Music will also reveal different personalities in me, therefore knowing other aspects of me as a person.

How does music speak to your heart? How do you think music has been influencing people's mindsets? How do you think music is affecting your communities and others?

Humble Beginnings

My mother's side of the family immigrated from Hong Kong to Toronto a few years before my mother conceived me. She is a very ambitious and hardworking woman who made sure she received her education (even though she would have to start over in her former career as a piano teacher) and worked non-stop to put food on the table. While my mother was constantly in college, my grandmother raised me up, so I spent the majority of my childhood with her, up until I gave birth to my third daughter.

I barely saw my mother, because of her studies, but whenever she had time, she would make sure she taught me different subjects and take me out super later into the city and parks. My grandmother and mom would teach me aspects of humanity, and also to enjoy the simple life and make the most out of it.

I grew up hearing plenty of jokes and remarks about Chinese families from other folks, like how every Chinese person was rich, etc. I never really took it in, because I didn't really care for materialistic things other than food and building blocks that I could use my imagination for. I was more interested in playing with rocks, watching bugs and digging up dirt, and was known for my imagination games. I got to play with my cousins' toys when they got bored of them or lent them to me. I remember envying a girl in class, because she got to pick up a chestnut, so during autumn I would always scavenge for a few before the squirrels got to them.

I lived with my extended family from infancy until early school days, and our family made sure we ate together, so we waited for everyone with the exception of mom, who came home around 9 pm. Mom was taking night courses, so Grandma would save a plate while everyone munched away. Being the person that she was, my grandmother would eat very little until everyone had their fill and finished what was left. Even though she encouraged me to eat, I would follow her footsteps and wait until everyone had left, and I would gobble up the remainder. Since it was the 6 of us at the dinner table and my cousins and uncle loved their meat, most of it would have been gone, so I ate the vegetables with Grandma. There were times when there wasn't enough, so my grandma would have salted duck eggs, preserved bean curd, or bamboo shoots to supplement. But we always saved money so that during Chinese festivals, especially Mid-Autumn and Chinese New Year, we would prepare food together as a family days before the festivals and have food lasting weeks after.

My grandma was raised in a small village back in China, and she brought her ways here. For example, washing clothes with a washboard and a big tub of water, sometimes having my cousin and I step in the bathtub filled with clothes to form a human washing machine. I used to watch my grandma hang the clothes outside and I would help her out and play with cousins, pretending we were on a mission into the jungle. My grandmother wanted to help our family save money, so she put in the extra work.

I felt the richest during my most humble times. The food tasted good even if it was canned mackerel with rice or hot dog and noodles. My family never made me feel I was poor; I was rich in my soul. My happiest times were just being with my family, and sometimes I wish we remained that way, but for the well-being of our living situations, I guess I have to accept that I am already blessed to have such a close relationship with my family.

When I started to make money, I went out more, and at one point was working so much that I never got to spend time to cook and eat with family. Even when I could afford to buy different things, I would rather go the plainer, simpler route. Deep down I wanted to maintain the life my grandmother raised me up in.

Even when I placed myself in difficult scenarios, I could always count on my family, even though I chose not to burden them too much. My grandmother saw many things, but she always had my back and she never told a soul. My cousins and I recently started to open up to each other and realized our own different paths from the same family tree. My uncle and aunt are more open and supportive than I thought, but I know they love me very much and I really do hope I can make it up for my family.

As the years passed and I started to do my own thing, I watched my family grow more distant from each other. But these memories are few of my main sources of joy during difficult times.

I barely speak about my childhood, but it was the humble beginnings I grew up in that have me cherish and appreciate the communities I will end up spending time to live or teach art education in. My humble beginnings are the reason why I continue to shower love to those I call my bigger family.

Year of The Full Bloom

Once upon a time
A little seed dropped from the sky.

Destiny soaring so high
The birds praised such a gift for the mortal world,
They started to cry.

Their drops of joy nourished the seed
As earth opened up to receive this heavenly prize.

A blanket presented by Helios
Delicately covered the seed
To shield The North Wind's might.

The seed grew from its humble home
Learning the ways of the land and water,
To love and respect creation
Frail or strong.

Years trickle away like petals of a withering rose,
Yet this seed continues to bloom each spring
More glorious than the year before.

The other majestic blossoms envied the seed
They couldn't bathe in their glory,
Therefore planted doubt inside like weeds.

The seed
Not knowing its full potential
Was confused...
Why hinder its growth
When there was no reason?

The seed continued to shine
Even when there was a time
Of pitch darkness.

It created new paths
Producing good fruits.
Even when dry spells
Threaten its existence.

As harvest became plentiful
The seed shared among her village.

No one shall starve
Or have little knowledge
For a feast and wisdom has been prepared among the
communal table.

The seed continues to break bread,
The seed is the most precious gift
Heaven has ever sent.

A heaven's jewel
Planted on earth,
To remain forever
Until the end of time.

Year of the full bloom
Has finally completed a life changing cycle.

Dedicated to Abena Offeh-Gyimah
My friend, sister and my inspiration to be a pursuer of my
dreams.

Killed 'Em With A Smile

Walk a day in my shoes
You will wonder why I haven't drowned in rhythm &
blues.

Walk a day in my shoes
You'll stop asking why I smile
Whenever there's a chance to.

They want to see the system break us down.
Feasting on our pains
To fill up their power lust.

They're scared to see us smile.
So fight back
By killing them with the brightest smile you got.

They want you to smile
When they see you frown.
They call you a sellout,
Once you smile a lot.

Because they intoxicate themselves
With reasons to remain down.
They want to receive the same strength
But their fear won't let them know how.

Social media creates envy
Depression
In the name of what?

Just as filters does wonders
Icons censor the times they have given up.

Everyone is happy until
Down time,
Then it's misery loves company
All around.

So don't take things so personal
Sometimes silence is better
And more effective
When you kill 'em with your brightest smile.

Behind These Walls

Glass Talks

Glass Talk 1

Her- Hey, how are you?

Him- *silence*

Her- I'm sorry, I haven't come visit you in a while.

Him- *silence*

Her- I was dealing with stuff.

Him- *silence*

Her- So... are you just going to sit here and not talk to me?

Him- *silence*

Her- It took me about 6 hours to get here. Please just say something! Anything!

Him- *silence*

Her- You want to call me names – go ahead! Rather that than nothing.

Him- *silence*

Her- *sigh* Look, I'm not here to argue, I can just leave.

Him- *quietly* What took you so long?

Her- Can't hear you, speak up!

Him- *quietly* What took you so long?

Her- Speak up.

Him- *Loudly* What FUCKING TOOK YOU SO LONG?

Other people including C.O. watches

Her- *nervously smiles and uses one hand to cover her face* I'm not trying to have our time get cut any shorter...

Him- Answer me!!!

C.O.- What seems to be the problem!

Him- Nothing sir, sorry.

C.O.- Keep it down before I cut this short, first and last warning! Have I made myself clear!!!!

Him- Yes sir.

C.O.- Hmph. *turns around*

Her- I told you I was busy.

Him- To even come check up on me. These demons could have killed me, and you wouldn't know.

Her- I'm... sor–

Him- Please just leave, you don't know what goes behind these walls. I needed you.

Her- I–

Him- Just go.

Her- Bye.

Glass Talk 2

A- Hey girl.

Z- What's up homie?

A- How are you doing these days?

Z- Trying to keep my head up.

A- That's good to hear, you almost done?

Z- Yeah…. How's everyone doing?

A- They okay.

Z- *stares at A for a bit* Tell me the truth.

A- *looks away* They fine.

Z- This not the time and place to lie to me.

A- *sigh* Most of them are doing fine.

Z- How's my dukes?

A- They doing way better now.

Z- They handling the bills?

A- I been helping them out.

Z- Thank you so much, I owe you.... How's Granny?

A- *looks down*

Z- How's Grandma... is she….

A- She been admitted into palliative care.

Z- *deep thought* The countdown.

A- Countdown?

Z- Yeah... I call it the countdown room…. How much longer?

A- The doctors said she only got this month.

Z- Only a month?

A- Yeah, that's the best they can do.

Z- But I'm coming out the first week of next month. Can't they prolong it?

A- They doing their best, but she can barely open her eyes.

Z- *mumbling to herself* Just a little longer…. Just a little…

A- I didn't want to tell you….

Z- I'm thankful you did… at least I can prepare myself right *sniff*

A- I'm really sorry… I….

Z- Look, I know you try to make things easier for me to swallow, but you already have by coming to see me, friend. Thank you for being my eyes and ears, thank you for checking up and taking care of my family. You are not obligated to, but you chose to take up the burden for being there for me. Seeing you helps me not feel like I'm left behind… no surprises *puts on a smile* no crazy news when I get out…. You never gave up on me even when my own family continued with their lives without me, I don't blame them, and I don't hate them for that. I guess I will never learn my lesson and make the same mistakes once I get out.

A- Don't say that, you're going to get your education and a job! I can help with your résumé and….

Z- I can't be saved, trust me….

A- But all those dreams you told me…

Z- Only dreams…. I'm a lost cause *looks at her somberly*…. *smiles* Enough of this emotional talk, I'll see you soon. Take care, friend, and make sure to get me a copy when you finish your project!

Glass Talk 3

Wife- I miss you!

Husband- I'm sorry.

Wife- For what?! You are an innocent man!!

Husband- I'm sorry for everything, I'm sorry that I had put you and our family through so much.

Wife- Stop apologizing, WE WILL get you OUT, you hear me!!!

Husband- They think I'm guilty, my love. You better off moving on with your life. I don't want to be a burden to our family anymore....

Wife- Did you drink that nasty concoction again? You must have lost your goddamn mind talking all that crazy shit!

Husband- I....

Wife- You better not give up on us, this is not your battle, this is our battle. God gives His greatest battles to His strongest people.

Husband- It has been 14 years already, 14 years too long.... I'm tired of fighting, I'm tired of this...

Wife- I need you, our son needs you....

Husband- I've failed him...

Wife- No you haven't, and you better stop talking like that before I come over there.... Don't test me.

Husband- *chuckles* Still haven't changed.

Wife- Your son is looking up to you, don't fail him now…. Show him that his father is a fighter... show him that in life there'll be hurdles that can be overcome.

Husband- I love you.

Wife- I love you too…. There's a lawyer that has been studying your case and is willing to take it up. Just hang in there.... I'll see you soon, baby. Please take good care of yourself.

Husband- I will, my love.

Glass Talk 4

T- Mommy, you believe me, right? You believe I didn't kill that man…

Mother- *glares and kisses teeth*

T- You really think I did it... Mommy….

Mother- Be a woman and own up to it. Stop crying wolf, my child.

T- Mommy! I didn't kill him, I didn't kill him!

Mother- Are you trying to tell me the officers framed you? Is that what you are trying to say?

T- I'm innocent, Mommy, I'm innocent....

Mother- *looks away in disgust* I thought you would've at least a bit of honour to know your wrongdoings... but I was proven wrong once again. I hope you learn your lesson and repent before you rot in hell.

T- Mommy... please believe me... please!

Mother- Enough of your insolence! I think it's best I give you some time to yourself before I come see you again.... *put the phone down and gets up*

T- *sobs* I'm innocent.... Mommy, please believe me.... Mommy, please.... believe me...

C.O.- Time's Up!! Wrap It Up!!!

Freedom of Lyricism

Lyrics for expression
Used as evidence during trials.

Does any other genre
Except hip hop and rap
Put their artists behind bars?

25 to life,
Babies raised in the pen
Yet can't use their pen to express.

Incarcerated for their words
While Politicians can openly disrespect the public.

They gave Ammo and G life
Dismissed their pleas
A Jury
Full of whites

Only words can get them locked up
Now everything is out of spite.

Some celebrate it as justice
But what's justice when verses become life sentences.

When evidence uses figures of speech
As confessions
This unreliable source can form more monsters than
helping them.

ICP
I don't see in penitentiaries

Freedom of Lyrics at its finest
How come they don't receive the same scrutiny.

'Cause you can't take words out of context
Can't assume or else all lyrics will solve cold cases.

Feeding prejudice won't equal fair judgement
There'll be no such thing as true freedom...

ICU

Cold hearted killers

Once I seen you in the ICU
I knew that they would murda you.
Pressuring granny to sign forms
Donating organs to other folks,
How come they didn't put that much passion into saving
    you.

Once I seen you in the ICU
I felt in my guts that they'll murda you.
They just as guilty as 1st degree
Cause they premeditated this shit,
But they walk away free
Since they got their diplomas and degrees,

Bubble in IV can easily bring demise
Don't think one's silence means being oblivious.
Stronghold sections
With some insiders who are demons,
How many loved ones could've been saved
If those who took up the vow were genuine.

When I seen you in the ICU
In my heart I already knew they would murda you.

Drugging you up as more stuff came up
We smell the stench of their lies,
Our regret was to allow them to admit you.

When I seen you in the ICU
I wanted to go in with you
'Cause I knew it would be my last,

My friend
In my heart I already knew they would murda you.

Behind These Walls

They told me to move forward... that they were a lost
cause... but I reminded them that they were also human...
that the world needed to hear their voices

Voice 1

I told her to abort it
Even though deep down I knew I'll regret because I was
    ecstatic when I found out she was pregnant.

My firstborn with my childhood sweetheart brought hope
    and joy.
Something I could look forward to when I come out
But I had to sabotage it.

I keep battling myself every day and night,
That's why I work out like an addict.
Instead of getting myself involved in unnecessary yard
    fights,
Or the hole amplifies my vision in pitch darkness.

I regret not having her keep my kid.
Sometimes I wish she would have done it behind my
    back.

Calling her names and let my rage fill...
While I dream of taking my child to doctor's
    appointments and boast when they become a grad.

She hated me
And stopped picking up my collects.
Put a halt in filling my canteen

But I'm not tripping,
Got my goons holding me down from the trap.

Won't blame her
If she resents me to her very last breath.
I was harsh when I put my foot down,
Instead of being honest that
I didn't want my child growing up without a dad.

She a strong woman
Who could provide with no one's help?
But my pride would not allow for my absence to be felt.

My eyes couldn't meet their eyes behind this glass.
The shame would make me break down
In front of demons behind these walls,
Can't afford that

I wish you could explain to her what I'm attempting to
    express.
Trusting your judgement to know when to have a heart to
    heart
Without her tryna break my neck.

Voice 2

I want to change
I want to be a no name.

I want to go about my day,
No hailing me up
Or someone trying to gain fame.

I want out of this mad house

Where I hear screams from lunatics
Wanting to drink human blood.

Can't even harm
These wicked guards....
Telling me
Canada....
Bring back death penalty
So they can fry my head off.

My cellmate going insane
His wife wants to call it quits.
Suspects she leaving him for some kid.

Sometimes I seek relief from a blade.
Or entice others to take my misery away
But I'm going to stay.

Being forced to be heartless
Then called a savage
What's the point of this game?

I write and draw
Counting the days left in this hell
I'm forced to see as my second home.

Voice 3

I want to thank the team for believing in me.
I want to thank you for all those times you wrote to me.

I thank you for seeing me as a human and not a scumbag
to society.

I am still human
Who made mistakes.
Some crimes I wish I could've took back
And those with no regrets,
It was for self defence
No guilt till my last breath.

I apologize to the family for the pain I caused,
I hope that next week would bring them closure.
I hope peace will bless their souls
Once and for all.

Tell my children
I will forever be with them.
When they miss me
They can speak to me through their prayers.
They will see me in their dreams
If they ask God often.

Tell my love
That there will always be a special place in this heart.

Our love has given me strength
During times
I wanted to do the executioner's job.
Our love has given me strength
To finish my last meal
Last shower
Last phone call.

Our love will continue to give strength
As I take my final steps
On this earth
And enter another chapter
For my soul.

This moment on
I'll enter the unknown.
From this moment on....
I'll know if I'm saved
Or cease to exist....

My loved ones
Please don't cry
And try to move on.

I love you all...

I am ready
You may proceed, Warden.

Voice 4

When I first got here
I wanted to get out so bad.
Got 7 years in this trash,
I couldn't wait to finish
To get back on track.

Heard horror stories from outside
That coming here
Was the end of my life.

Yet as I learned how to talk the talk
And walk the walk
Learned how to adapt....
I'm starting to see outside as the junkyard
This is no man's land
This is where I belong....

I met some who'll spend their last days
And some who were never trill at all.

I met some who fell into lust
And ones who never been solid
Just have to know the community behind these walls.

Who said I am suffering for losing freedom
When we are all in the same boat.

Same positions
Rules and regulations....
Except you outsiders are stuck in the matrix
Snap out!
Stay woke!!

Voice 5

A true mother's love
Will never end.
Protecting her offspring
No matter how messed up they been.

Maybe too nurturing for her children's good,
But the only woman worthy to depend and show love to.

Mother gave birth and is the only one
Who can take it away?

The state wants to have a final say,
But it's a true mother's love
That will tend to all wounds sustained.

Voice 6

Why am I being left alone?
In a place where I don't belong.

Why are these days becoming longer than before?
I stare at the cold door.

Why won't they hear my pleas of innocence?
They just need to give me a chance to speak.

I waited days to months and now years
For a trial
That seems to be pushed back...

I refuse to die in here.

Please

Give me that one chance.

Voice 7

Behind these walls
I know who's real and who's not.

Behind these walls
Even the most feared monsters
Have more heart
Than most.

They were the ones that had my back
The only ones I can rely.
Tended to my wounds

Split meals
And my
Guidance.

Just for some extra pay
Ones who were hired to protect...
Forget their jobs for a sec,
It was the set that risked their lives to defend.

It wasn't these uniformed fake heroes
That gave a damn.

Labelled as God's mistakes
Maybe it is the ones who are not here
That are the real demonic worship.

Voice 8

My eyes cannot unsee
My nose cannot forget the stench.

My hands continue to be covered with rotten flesh
Because of what Your Majesty put me as.

My ear still ripples in shell shock
Wishing the drums would collapse.
At least this sacrifice be the price
For sleeping well for many nights.

My tastebuds shiver
Yet my lips and throat are forced
To be deceitful.

My instincts became so in tune

191

That when I'm out
I'll claw
So no surprises
Don't forget to knock on the door.

Cries of The Ghetto

Ghetto Gospel

I remember I had to bury my homie at 15
Always knew him as an angel
But he lived a sinner's dream.

Ambitions and Goals splattered on concrete
Right from behind
That's why
I pray cleansing of foes from family.

I look up to the sky
On my knees
Rain kissed my cheeks.
Begging the Lord why
Why He refuse to speak.

At that moment
It's been a while
Questioning His Ways with me

Turn my back from the grave
Before I lose my sanity

Stuck at the Crossroad.

I've attended more Sunsets than Sunrises

Gunshot

Death became a norm
News chattering all day long.

Like leaves during the fall
Bodies be dropping on the floor.

All the children hear are sirens
Having family security crumbling.

Having mothers always asking
Do you know this or that person.

Hot streaks but it won't mean nothing
Women of steel continue to do their life stealing.

Click Clack!!
Continue their mission
Cold heart with their own ambitions.

Motive driven
Blood seeking visions.

Don't care who suffer
From the aftermath explosion.

See why people avoid negativity
Lying to themselves
That the world is ONLY filled with positivity.

You can hide
And you can run.
Blood seeping through the cracks
Even touching sheltered ones.

Death hitting close to home
Demand justice
But will receive none.

Till unity
There won't be peace.
Only way to redeem
Is for the gun production to come to cease.

Wrong Place, Wrong Time

Restless spirits
Wandering restless nights,
Time cut short
Screaming Why
        Why
            Why!!!!!!

And they ain't do nothing
Why they gotta pay the price?

Some unlucky souls
That got caught up
At the wrong place
At the wrong time.

Guilty by association
Catching off guard

Luring the big fish
By taking out bait from the crowd.

Fallen Soldier

The hood
Will never be the same
Lost a Real G in the game
Whole block is going insane.

True soldier at birth
Now rest in peace from earth,

Your legacy will continue
And your voice shall be heard.

Liquor
Pour out to good friend

Family will miss,
But never forget,
An honest man.

The Skies have taken care
There's no more suffering....

That came to an end.

(hook)

Can you hear me, baby
Watch my baby,
Will you hold us down from up there?

It's getting crazy...
Right here.
And it's insane...
Everywhere (x2)

Bad Habits

"Two double shots of tequila, please," Rose asked a bartender who had been serving her throughout the night.

"Damn girl, I wish I could drink like you," the bartender replied as she poured out the drinks and served it to her.

"Haha, no, you don't, love…. It's a curse, haha." Rose tried to laugh it off.

She meant every word and felt a jab inside her heart. You see, Rose was never the girl who drank for fun or even went out to parties or bars a lot. But since her grandmother and her recent loss of an unborn child, she had been going berserk. She hated the fact she stopped cringing when she tasted overproof alcohol. She hated those days when she almost bought up the whole bar, yet she could still take a couple of buses and walk all the way home. She hated those nights when her body was exhausted and was about to burst into alcohol poisoning, but her heart wanted to chug more. Rose started to collect receipts from the liquor stores and bars to just snap her back into reality about where her money was going, when she could have been saving a fortune because most of her expenses went to her wants instead of her needs.

"The hell are you doing drinking so late by yourself?" a former lover once told her.

"You acting like you a fiend," another one yelled at her when she FaceTimed him.

"What's really going on with you, talk to me," a local of the bar used to try to ask.

Even if their intentions were good and genuine, Rose would bark back with no hesitation. Not too long ago she tried to explain that her grief can be overwhelming and that drinking helped her to sleep. Maybe it was because she was a woman that people didn't believe her and assumed it was relationship problems or loneliness. The locals used to bother her by asking where she lived, or how's her love life, until one day she had enough and almost started a bar fight over a local's smart remark. Rose made sure she would never drink to the point she became forgetful, and remember which questions were constantly asked and had her guard up.

She was super productive during the day no matter how much she drank the day before. She was able to carry her duties at work with ease and was able to cook and do errands back home. She was able to promote and support her friends' events and seemed to look like everything was fine. It wasn't until super late at night when everyone in her household was sleeping, that she had to fight out the temptations to not stay sober.

When Rose just found out her good friend's grandmother passed, she started to head over to a local bar and order a pint of beer. Two weeks after, her own grandmother told her how her doctor mentioned about her impending doom for rejecting a life-saving surgery. Her grandmother was in her 90s, so she took into consideration the risks of doing surgery at such an old age; she chose the natural way of dying. Rose started to order two pints and went drinking with her friends so she could order pitchers. When she was by herself, she found that beer wasn't cutting it for her, so she upgraded to drinking hard liquor. That's when she found herself bar hopping and experimenting with different mixes to satisfy her need to be intoxicated. Eventually she became a regular, so the others started to enter her personal space, which depended on her mood that day, if she was going to converse or attempt to throw an object across the bar. The regulars learned to read her body language and warned others who seemed to be overstepping her boundaries.

She has stopped for a good amount of time but eventually, she recently picked up the habit again when she lost a child. It was either she would become an untameable force of destruction or find ways to numb her pain.

She just didn't know how to cry for help, because she was raised up in a way where issues were kept within her family. Her grandmother was her heart and whatever bothered Rose, she would run to her and spill everything. But with the absence of a mighty spirit, Rose's heart unleashed the chilling voices of her internal asylum that were threatening her whole existence.

Deep down she knew that this path was not for her. She could smoke and drink her sorrows away, but it was just brushing them under the rug, eating away valuable money and promoting an early end.

Rose knew she would have to heal from this and face everything head on.

Rose needed to break the cycle of bad habits.

Get To Know

Didn't see him as a Menace
Only known him as a friend.
Putting food on the table
Children crying at an empty fridge.
No luck in finding a job
Though more qualified than the rest.
But which job would pick a criminal,
Over a clear record,
Ones that haven't gotten caught yet.

Or that brilliant graduate from the block
That wants to contribute towards society,
Her curse was where she rested each night
Rejections slapping away her dignity.

The one that was like a sister
Selling her body to pay her rent,
No one listened to her cries from molestation
Had no choice other than to flee.

In solitude
Is the one time they can reflect,
Outcasts and the shunned.
Their only hope
Is finding peace with their present and past.

Surviving today to see tomorrow
Every decision to make amends.

Outsiders don't know…
But they judge most
Talk the most smack.

They praise theories
In perfect scenarios,
Excluding other factors
The reality of what life throws.

Outsiders can only see the cover,
Only the insiders know what's best
Behind those hardened doors.

Come Back Home

Late night missions
Got her trippin'.

Carrying his child in her womb,
Prays that God won't make
Another child
Fatherless.

She had begged him
To not go,
But he refused
With dollar signs in his burning eyes.

"I won't allow my family to go hungry,
Or I had failed to provide."

He walks
In
And
Out.

Having her beg
But it goes in
One ear
And out.

The news lists out descriptions and names…
Each time she fears it'll be him.

At night
He steps out...
She is blocking the door
Refusing to let him out.

"My spirit is telling me you need to stay home"
She cries,
Even though he tries to brush her aside.

"Don't go!"
          "I'll be back home soon"
"Something is not right"
          "You say that every night"

He walks out the door
Kissing her goodbye....
"Get ready for some love making tonight"

She watches him walk away
As she whispers
"Come back home, my love"

And that was the last time
She saw....
Him.

Come back home my sweet darling
Come back home to me love.

Why did you not listen...?
Listen to the warnings that night.

Come back home my sweet darling
I need you right here.

Another cold case
After so many years....

Haunting Me

Watched my boy's youngest daughter
Had to bury her father.
All in the name of a block
That won't deal with his grave proper.

Only a distant memory
Now I'd watch his daughter get bitter.
She wants justice for her Pops,
I see the hatred consume her.

The law failed her many times
Now the streets had an offer.
Sell her soul to the gang
They'll make sure
To eliminate his killa.

She kept debating
Hesitating
But this rage won't subside.
Got too deep into the game
She lived and died by the gun.

Now in just a few weeks
She'll rest by his side.
He comes inside my dreams
And all he does
Is breaks down and cries.

"I failed, Glow
I failed, Glow
I failed as a father,
I let greed take over
I forgot to protect my one and only daughter"

I told him it's not only him
Maybe I failed as an aunt.
She watched me fight with my inner demons,
She saw my eyes of revenge.

I should have sought help with my pain
Instead I masked myself in anger.
Started to be a different monster

Crying was weakness
To me when I was a lot younger.

Caught up in my feelings,
Didn't see her becoming a heartless person.

Now what I see in my dreams
Are two souls trapped.
But it's daughter like father.

Hood Chronicles Song List – Part III

Blacus Ninjah - Make It Through
Boosie Badazz - Mama Know Love
Saigon Feat. Trey Songz - Pain IN My Life
Papa Duck - In The Hood
Trill Fam - Where Would I Be
Pinky - Backbone
Blood Raw - Cries Of The Ghetto
Lola Bunz - Hood Life
J Noble Feat. Golde London - Who We Be
Kilo Shomari - Untitled
Ice Cube - Why We Thugs
Jadakiss Feat. Anthony Hamilton - Why
Spin El Poeta - To All My Boyz In The Hood
Collie Buddz - Come Around
Shortiie Raw - Love Got Me
Casey K Jonesz - Lessons
Sedrik - VRS
Plies - Somebody Loves You
Littles Feat. Ammo - Stressful Times
Baby Grhyme - Ain't Nothing Pretty
Nathan Baya - Reasons To Grind
Mad Linqz - Survivor
Csin - Been Grinding Since I Came Out
Alicia Cinnamon - I Can't Breathe
Young Buck - Prices On My Head
Star Dat Prince - Circle Of Pain
Shortiie Raw Feat. Molly Brazy - Drip
TMC McCrea - Pain
Uncle B-NO x Csin x TallSick - Newz
Rhonda - Jah Jah Protect Me
Ammo - Never Look Back
Young Jeezy Feat. Keyshia Cole - Dreamin
Boosie Badazz - Mind Of A Manic

What The Media Won't Show

#SupportLocalBeforeGlobal

Nathan Baya, founder of JaneStreetSpeaks, created this hashtag around 2018.

"Support Local Before Global means to support from the bottom and not waiting till they reach the top to uplift them, 'cause you didn't raise someone up, if you waited until they reach the top to extend your hand." – Nathan Baya

#SupportLocalBeforeGlobal – Be sure to follow the hashtag on your social media and to include it when sharing your friends and fellow residents' dreams.

Here are only a few (I mean a sprinkle) of the initiatives, events, etc. in the GTA (Greater Toronto Area) that focuses on providing support for a number of needs in the communities (such as mental health, nutrition, criminal justice, politics, education, arts, etc.). I am encouraging all of you to take your time to look up impactful initiatives. Also, please go beyond this list and discover more hidden gems in this city. Don't forget to share this community wealth with loved ones.

- **One Mic Educators**
- **The H.O.P.E (Helping Offenders on Probation Excel) Program**
- **#TheHopeInThe6ix**
- **JaneStreetSpeaks**
- **Olori Jane and Finch**
- **Adda Blooms**
- **Trinity Connects**
- **Black Creek Farm**
- **Strive Toronto**
- **Black Light Focus**

- **Activated Podcast**
- **SYLC Radio**
- **MorningStar Printing**
- **Round My Block**
- **Reclaim Your Voice**
- **R.I.S.E Edutainment**
- **Word Spell TO**
- **Kapostrophe Media**
- **Dear Self Love**
- **R1ders 1st ENT**
- **Sundae Doodles**
- **Cr8tive Eye**
- **Miss H's Workshop**
- **Credon Studios**
- **Wheel It Studios**
- **WWETV Worldwide**
- **Heart Summer Festival**
- **RayCreatesArt**
- **Haprit Gill Money Talks**
- **Black Community Love**
- **CEE Centre For Young Black Professionals**
- **Vibe Arts TO**
- **ArtReach**
- **Urban Arts TO**
- **Rhythm & Soul Thursdays**
- **DevelopMe Youth**
- **Clean & Shine Car Detailing**
- **Tea Base**
- **Think2wice**
- **Morgridge Foundation**
- **Writing While Black**
- **Jane Finch Bee**

Flower Of Resistance

Each distinctive design reveals tales
Petal by petal.

Even between the small cracks
Of the sun-baked concrete,
This sturdy flower pushes through.

Showering peace to all its surroundings,
No one could see the scars
As they only saw a rejuvenating being.

Pollinating hope
Through messengers from the kingdom of earth.
The flower watches in humbled awe,
While drenched in the storms
It continued to fight for the light to re-emerge.

A flower so potent with love,
It spreads throughout the rainforest
To be enjoyed by all.

A story that will continue to thrive
Through it all.
This flower will continue to share its story…
Petal...
By…
Petal….
Even when the time has come to cease,
The flower's legacy will live on.

Dedicated to Jungle Flower

Land of Prosperity

Dedicated to Shadoozy

A Nubian king displays his ancestral crown
Stretching down his back.
Each loc mapping his kingdom
Gifting clues,
For wisdom and mystery to flourish
Beyond little minds to comprehend.

Or so he thought

The young followed the king's footprints in the sand,
Did not speak,
Ears open,
Learning,
Teachings saturate their heads.

His words may be hard to swallow at first,
Yet they are sweet as honey in the end.

His reign is full of music and laughter,
His people danced away in all kinds of weather.

Taking in children underneath the protection of his
wings,
The king welcomed and adopted nations into his palace.
A gesture only The Greats would understand.

Father's Day

Like the fire disk waltzing amongst Celestial realms
Awakening Madre Terra,
He is the epiphany of his household.

He is like a shepherd of a hundred lambs
Fending off danger
Even if it's with a wooden staff.

He protects his bloodline like a cup-bearer
Tasting the first royal wine
His cup overflows with loyalty and strength.

Even receiving compliments and thanks
Numerous as grains of sand,
It can never comprehend.

This gratitude,
Rejoicing parenthood before and after
This universal day.

For a father's role will never come to cease.

A father will be a father for lifetimes and can never be
replaced.

*Dedicated and inspired by an amazing person that had
entered my life pouring endless blessings. You are
appreciated and cherished by your family and friends for
the rest of your days. I love you and I thank you. Thank
you for being who you are.*

To all the fathers and father figures that continue to play
a huge part in our communities,
You are loved and your worth is indescribable.
Your presence....
Irreplaceable.

Mama G

In memory of Doreen Edwards, August 22,1922 – June 29, 2016

"Sweetie, your breakfast is ready, don't wait for it to go cold!" A strong Caribbean accent woke Aretha out of her light sleep. She yawned and rubbed her eyes before getting up to pull up the curtains in the room. She pushed the stubborn windows up to allow the cool fresh breeze to fill her room. The spring wind woke her fully as it sent chills down her spine. She trembled as she opened up the closet to pick the clothes she will wear for today.

Aretha walked up a short flight of stairs to the living room, greeting everyone along the way. A hot plate of ackee and saltfish with some fried dumplings, bowl of callaloo, and a cup of water greeted her on a hand-carved table and two wooden chairs. She could smell the Manish water cooking in the kitchen and stuck her head to the side to peek at what other delights were being prepared for supper later on. It was Sunday morning, and everyone in the household had pitched in during the week so they could have a feast – it was a household tradition.

"Good morning, mom," Aretha greeted the lady who was cooking in the kitchen before devouring her meal.

Dionne Patterson was her name, but everyone called her "mom" or "Mama G." Mrs. Patterson was seen as the hood mom by everyone in the neighbourhood. She was stocky, about 5 foot 5 with a dullish grey afro and rich dark brown skin. Her wrinkles were barely visible, but if you look closely, you can see wisdom spread across her hands and face.

216

Mrs. Patterson took in all the kids that were abandoned, disowned and living in the streets. She had a two-storey, 3-bedroom suite in a housing complex by Jane and Finch. She had been living in the area since she immigrated from Kingston, Jamaica in the early '50s and had never left. She was married to her late husband for 43 years before he passed away recently due to natural causes; they did not have any children. She had seen the good and the bad, with people coming and going over the years, and had raised up a majority of the folks there. Everyone came to her for advice and shelter, and her cooking had people from all over the city to taste her dishes.

Aretha recently got into an ugly argument with her mother and ran away. She spent weeks couch surfing at different places. One of the guys on the block noticed her and took her to Mrs. Patterson, and it was her most stable living condition for several months now. Aretha made sure to buy her own bedsheets and pillow casings and groceries, so she wouldn't be a burden. She would also help Mrs. Patterson with errands for the house and cook.

The house was always lively and there wasn't much time for solitude. Aretha was accustomed to this from her growing up in a big household, and she preferred it that way. She kept much to herself, occupying her time with journaling, painting and odd jobs. During the times she had no work, she would forage for liquor bottles in order to make some chump change from the stores. Aretha was offered some narcotics one time, and she wanted to start selling them to make some income, but Mrs. Patterson discovered them and flushed them down the toilet before sitting Aretha down for a heart-to-heart talk. Aretha had expected to be banned, since it was the very same reason that caused her and her mom to fall out. But instead Mrs.

Patterson shared about her personal experiences as a former drug dealer, and they became inseparable since.

Aretha eventually put down her walls and opened up more to Mrs. Patterson as time passed. Mrs. Patterson never judged her and showed her unconditional love. Aretha had maintained contact with her mother since Mrs. Patterson convinced her to. She would call and visit her family every weekend before going back to Mrs. Patterson's. Her mother kept a decent relationship with Mrs. Patterson and would be updated on Aretha's progress.

Aretha finally moved back in with her mom but would constantly call and visit Mrs. Patterson, and even slept over once in a while. She watched Mrs. Patterson age, but her spirit was youthful as ever. When Aretha started to go back to school and was doing placements, pursuing a second career through her art, she would always return to share the good news to Mrs. Patterson. There was a time when Aretha was selling her artwork at a local market, and Mrs. Patterson went by her booth and wanted to purchase her painting. Aretha offered a discounted rate, but Mrs. Patterson wasn't having it.

"Pickney, how much is it; I'm buying full price and nothing less, you hear!" Mrs. Patterson would scold while lecturing Aretha about valuing her hard work.

Mrs. Patterson had always supported Aretha to the best of her ability, purchasing her artwork even when she wanted to present them as a gift.

Mrs. Patterson passed away at a ripe old age, still standing strong and independent until her very last breath. Aretha and a small group of loved ones were by her deathbed. Mrs.

Patterson had given them instructions and bid farewell before sending them out the room; she wanted to be in peace by herself. After dealing with funeral and burial matters, Aretha, alongside her two close friends, went to clean up Mrs. Patterson's apartment. She stayed back a bit later and went into Mrs. Patterson's drawer, opening the lock with the key. Mrs. Patterson had given her the key during her last days.

When Aretha opened up the drawer and searched through the contents, she picked up folders, notebooks and sketchbooks before sitting on the edge of Mrs. Patterson's old bed. She flipped through sketchbooks, each page more breathtaking than the other, with drawings of phoenixes, trees, oceans, mountains and much more. Each page had Mrs. Patterson's signature and was dated when it first started and finished, along with an inspiration note. Aretha read the poetry and was in awe of Mrs. Patterson's talent.

"How come she kept this to herself all this time?" Aretha said out loud as she went through the poetry. The last book had a musty scent and a beautiful furnished wood cover, with ancient decorative paper inside. Suddenly an envelope dropped onto Aretha's lap. She opened the envelope which had a few letters inside in good condition. This implied that it was written not a long time ago. It had beautiful handwritten words, and she read the letter out loud:

April 7th, 2013

To My Favourite Sweetheart,

Now that I have finally reunited with Our Lord Saviour, I can finally worship for His Majesty. I hope you will be cooking at home more instead of take-outs, because I will make sure Jesus will send me back to give you lashes; don't play with me. Sweetie, don't be sad but you must rejoice and live your life to the fullest. I know you well enough to know that you putting up a front and you must cry it out, don't hold nothing back, bad for your health. That what happen to me ever since my sweet Errol left. I was heartbroken hoping that helping our community would fill the void, yet grief prevailed, and my body is giving up. The doctor told me I had only a year left, but I will prove him wrong, I can't leave everyone just yet, I still have to finish my recipe book. Yes Aretha, I am putting all your favourite dishes in it. I thought it was best since I won't be able to fill your belly up no more.

Surprise!!! I left you a few farewell presents, I hope you like them.

Dionne Patterson

Aretha held the book and carefully looked through the recipes and smiled. She started to go through the other letters, which were dedicated to Mrs. Patterson's friends and other children. Aretha organized the letters into envelopes and put them in her backpack. She had one more letter for herself and started to read it slowly. Her eyes began to water up as she read it out loud:

April 7th, 2016

To My Darling,

I know my time is near, I felt it when I was going for my morning stroll by the creek. I will miss you all, especially you, Aretha. Aretha, I never had to worry about you. I know you will thrive and do well for yourself and your children.

People may have called you names, looked down on you and overlooked your greatness. I believe in what you are capable of. You had dealt with a lot of trials, and I must say you are my inspiration. Aretha, you will know when you are ready to share your art to the world. When you do, don't ever look back. You may have doubted your talent because you aren't receiving the recognition, but all shall know your worth. You must believe in yourself. The world needs to know your story; your story had a positive impact on my life. I am honoured to have been part of your journey. What you had shown the world is only a fragment of your light. The pieces you recited, you must share with the world when the time is right.

Don't hold back any longer, Aretha. The art pieces that you will see are pieces that I wrote and drew throughout my life. I held back my God-given gift, because no one took me seriously except my sweet Errol who continued to invest in me. It was because of witnessing your passion that motivated me to draw once again. Don't you dare settle for less; continue to push! Even though I won't be physically with you, my spirit shall continue to be the other set of footprints in the sand. I love you, Aretha. Until we meet again,

Dionne Patterson

Aretha put the letter down before her tears soaked the fragile paper. She started to wail as she clenched her fists, covering her eyes. She had not shed a tear at all when they sent Mrs. Patterson's body back to her hometown in Jamaica. Aretha had become a workaholic to contribute to the funeral costs and to distract her mind. Her lips craved the taste of the liquor but held back until Mrs. Patterson was buried in the ground and to clear any debts. She felt her heavy heart become lighter as she drained herself out until she fell into a deep sleep.

"Suga plum," a voice sweet as nectar filled up Aretha's ear drums.

"Mama G? Where are you, I can't see you!" Aretha shouted, her voice echoing into the lush rainforest.

It was spitting rain and thick fog was making it hard to see anything on the ground.

"Come here, my child." Mrs. Patterson's voice came from the heavens above in the canopy.

Aretha looked up at this mighty tree, and she saw liana vines intertwining from the ground to beyond the sky. She started to climb it, way up high, passing the clouds until her feet stepped onto a platform made of gold. Once Aretha finally got on top of the platform, she found herself standing on a road made out of white gold. At the end of the road was a mighty clear crystal gate, encrusted with every jewel you can think of, and with gold loop handles. There was a stream on her left side that had colours of sunset, while on her right were trees producing every kind of fruit. Two enormous eagles came from the sea of clouds and sang their songs as they circled around Aretha. Then three doves joined the eagles in their song as Aretha witnessed their spectacular performance. Then one of the doves landed on the palm of her hand and cried out diamond tears, and the drops started to meld together till they became a medallion.

"Go to the gate, my child." The birds spoke in unison in the voice of Mrs. Patterson.

Aretha started to walk towards the gate and when she stood in front of the structure, the two mighty eagles stood on each side of the gate and the three doves stood in front of Aretha. One eagle opened its mouth, and out came a spider made of sapphire and it crawled up from Aretha's legs to her palm and spun out three diamond threads on three sides of the medallion, forming a trinity with loose ends on each side before crawling back into the eagle's mouth. The three doves flew to Aretha. Each bird picked one of the three loose strands of the medallion and together, they placed the medallion into an empty circular slot right in the middle of the door handles. Once inserted, there was a flash of light before the gates slowly opened. Aretha had to cover her eyes from the light, and when she slowly opened her eyes, she saw Mrs. Patterson in a long dark purple dress with gold slipper orchid designs all over. Mrs. Patterson was glowing like the sun, and when she smiled her teeth were as white as snow. Her crown was made of lily stargazers, and she was holding a bunch of lignum vitae flowers. Mrs. Patterson didn't say anything as she continued to smile at Aretha.

"I love you, Aretha, my sweet dawta," Mrs. Patterson said as she walked up to Aretha and embraced her tightly.

"I love you, my sweet angel." Mrs. Patterson bid her farewell before disappearing into thin air.

Aretha woke up to the rays of sun that pierced inside the room. She rubbed her eyes and stretched before she finally finished up clearing out the place. She wrote down her dream and made a collection with all of Mrs. Patterson's artwork and written work.

A few years after Mrs. Patterson's passing, Aretha decided to showcase Mrs. Patterson's art. With the proceeds, she decided to fund a mobile social supermarket in the Jane and Finch area. This is where families who are struggling can purchase produce at an affordable rate that's under market value and learn essential life skills such as budgeting and cooking. Mrs. Patterson had taken in orphans and children who were disowned. One particular orphan became a professor, and his teaching influenced many more youth to build up a passion for social justice in their communities. Plenty of the children that Mrs. Patterson raised up became successful in various careers, especially the orphans. Together, they supported Aretha's vision of continuing Mrs. Patterson's legacy and good works, through education, financial literacy, food security and much more.

I want to take the time to give thanks for the ones that took me in and treated me as if I am one of their own. Thank you for playing an essential part in our communities and raising us all. Gems within our hoods that will touch the hearts of many. I love you all and I continue to be grateful for each and every one of you.
- Glowz

Street 101

Street Life

Streets showed me no matter how many times we try to
prevent,
YGs will make the same mistakes as the olderheads...
But we still preach.

Every man for themselves behind interrogation room.
Life sentence thrown
Lips jump
Even when they supposed to be sealed.
(Freedom more valued than loyalty)

Set ups will never come to cease,
It's like every person from the block is a friend, hidden
enemies.

Temporary pleasures must been worth the risk,
Shoulda took your eyes out
Now mans be carrying you in a garbage bag. (Aint that
shit)

Time doesn't mean anything
3 shots to the dome from the back
"Isn't that their road dawg, what's he doing here"

Better watch out for those quiet ones
Real Gs moves in silence
No need to brag
Obtain a record to be a big boss. (Take notes)

Got a big ego
Might as well invest into getting strapped up.
Make sure you got eyes on all sides
Decrease probability to slip up.

Being flashy
Only attracts fake love
Unwanted attention.
Remove that mask with makeup remover
Witness a magic trick from the audience

Can't be too much of a hothead
Hotheads get plunged to cool off,
There a time and a place
So chill and observe before hyping up on the spot.

Street life ain't for everybody
Easy to decipher when the guns go off.

'Bout that life
Till it hits home
Now watch them
Protesting to stop.

Kids killing kids
Over reasons they probably don't know about.

That same bus route got you entering enemy turf
Covering your face at bus stops.

Blood spill for same factors
But that's what street life is about.

Where Are You From?

Where are you from?
Starting to hate being asked that question.

Sometimes
Refrain myself from asking someone else,
So they won't feel uptight with the block they're from.

Maybe it's my innocence.
Maybe I just can't travel around
Without being harassed.

Maybe because I love one side more…
I shouldn't be anywhere near the other side
Or am I sentencing myself to death?

Maybe it's the predatory instincts
That urge them to stalk me.
Waiting at my home
For the perfect chance to pounce me!

Undressing me with their eyes…
Is that why they keep asking?

They don't know
But I love to explore.
No restrictions I place on myself
In this city I call home.

And you would have thought
That their street smarts
Would realize
Don't shit where you made your bed….

But common sense went out the door!

Is it because I am not my counterparts?
Misogyny got them assuming
I'm gullible!

Or worry who I know
Because bad mind can't sleep
With all the sinister deeds they caused.

Sins haunting their surroundings
Causing them to want to scan everyone's households.

Does it irk their aura?
Does my spirit taunt their paranoia?
Questions I ask myself…
When I sit down and reflect.

But be wary
How often you've asked me….
Where I'm from.
You know if it was the mandem
You be prime suspect on their hit list.

Don't say I never told you so.

The question can open a can of worms
You're not prepared to handle.

Art of War

"If you know the enemy and know yourself, you need not fear the result of a hundred battles. If you know yourself but not the enemy, for every victory gained you will also suffer a defeat. If you know neither the enemy nor yourself, you will succumb in every battle."
— **Sun Tzu**, *The Art of War*

My mother and I grew up watching different historical-based dramas from China and Korea. I have an interest in war-based drama series and the use of literature based on *The Art Of War* by Sun Tzu, which talks about different perspectives and battle tactics used in war. I wanted to explore this area with my own twist and share some of my thoughts. I will touch upon a few things, and disclaimer: these are just my opinions from my own lived experiences. Life is full of different roads, so not one road is the right way. I want to share with you, my readers, words and some insights that I'd wish to have told my younger self, as well as my older and younger friends from the communities I grew to love.

Knowledge Is Power

Being equipped in knowledge is powerful. My mother always said that people can take away your pride, discriminate you, etc., but they can never take away your wisdom. Though the road may be rough, the knowledge you feed yourself with will take you to places that nobody would've thought imaginable. Some older folks would tell me that when they started their crews during school days, each member had to maintain their grades to no less than 90 percent. There were severe consequences if academic success was not achieved, such as beating and being banned from the crew. I looked up to how they would make it a priority to give their children the best education, schools and to have tutors to ensure success. Now if the children decide to make the most out of these tools or walk their own path – that is another story.

Twisted Law

I remember when I used to attend cookouts and gatherings, surrounded by folks from different walks of life. They would talk about how back in the day, in order to even get into a crew, you had to have read the whole entire law book and must stay updated with domestic and international laws since it constantly changed, which would open up more loopholes that can be discovered and used. I also remember I had an interest looking into cartels, mafia and other criminal organizations on how they operated, and how they were able to stay away from the watchful eyes of the public for so long. I noticed there were a few things in common, such as having some connections with law enforcement or people with big influence such as judges and politicians. They would have friends and associates who had clear records that no one would suspect, until years after, that would be within their circle.

Notorious enforcers who were also being FBI informants captured my attention, "assisting" the law in order to avoid harsh sentences, then be disposed for "justice" when they were no longer of use, or when they had "went too far" for the law to turn a blind eye. Witnessing the distortion of justice being carried out made me question how easy it was to manipulate the system, and how sometimes it was better to represent yourself to get out of the vicious cycle of the twisted law.

Knowing Your Enemy

We put most of our focus on visible oppositions and assume the enemies at work are people such as residents from rivalling neighbourhoods, law enforcement, killers, snitches, drug users, friends who envy and are jealous, etc.

Yet we barely take notice of and brush off things like greed, anger that is masking depression, trauma and grief. Prosecutors and defence lawyers who would still go out for recess and laugh at the case together while they still get paid – to them in most cases, it's just business.

Not to mention, wording used in courts often pit people against one another, which causes some folks to be quick to defend themselves without having the emotional strength to wait to receive the full disclosure.

And have I mentioned retaliation on "snitches" without getting that paperwork?

A big enemy I had witnessed and experienced myself way too often is being loyal to a fault. This loyalty in theory is what everyone dreams of, demanding that their circle to be like that. Yet this hidden enemy has cost lives and the well-being of people for thousands of years, yet it still continues with denial not far behind.

Emotions when not balanced properly can be a destructive force that cannot be reckoned with.

Enemies that we have to be wary of are the ones that know too much about our inner core while we look past them.

Conclusion

"So in war, the way is to avoid what is strong, and strike at what is weak."
— **Sun Tzu**, *The Art of War*

The art of war I personally define does not focus on warfare. I believe it teaches discipline, mercy, wisdom, education and most of all – peace. War is not always on the outskirts as it can start within the inner walls of yourself. War and bloodshed will bring downfall to prosperity, so why not celebrate when the days are good, instead of troubling yourself with little quarrels? The real hunger will have you yearning for peace instead of making a name for yourself far greater than what you need. Earning stripes will make you a prime target eventually and being a terror in the streets will have bystanders watching and laughing as you suffer and cry for help. Staying low is the key!

What are your thoughts about this piece? Jot it down and discuss amongst yourselves and reflect. What are some parts you took in or would love to add? Were some of these concepts familiar to you, or something you never thought about before? Are there some segments you want more clarification on? Hit me up in person or on social media and let's talk!

Peace & Love
-Glowz

Ryders

Where Day 1's when shit hits the fan
Ryders turn drive by when given insights from the pen.

Your OPPs in full focus
But your back has no lens,
Buried my niggas scattered in pieces
By their so-called friends.

They say blood is thicker
Than water
Guess mine got diluted.

Shot my nigga D
Had him run.
His asthma finished what they started (Now I'm livid.)

Classmates killing classmates
Over money, disses and whores,
Starving don't mean loyalty
When baby moms give the best dome.

They claim to be your ryder
So they can scope you out,
Blueprinting your next moves
So they can catch you off.

My OG biggest mistake
Was not being Solo.
Trusted his goons
Now he won't be able to see tomorrow. (Such a Sorrow)
Real niggas rolling in their graves
If they heard what was being said,
What has become of their cliques

Why niggas so quick to drop their sets.

If spirits were allowed to roam
It's game over.
Mandem go berserk
From guilty conscience
Of the whispers.

Everyone claims to be a ryder
Until it's time to put in work.
Everyone claims to be a ryder
Until Feds slap time that'll be served.

Everyone claims to be a ryder
Until their sins catch up to murk.

You are your own best ryder
If there's anything that can be learnt.

Inspired by Heartless G – It's On

Bwoy Dem

Protectors, pigs, 5-0, sheriff, bwoy dem, undercovers, peace officers, heroes, bacon, Babylon, and the list goes on and on. How they are viewed, respected and labelled varies case by case, taking into consideration the key factors of neighbourhoods, carding, interactions and skin tone, which can affect how the other party would view them.

There is a significant amount of differences and separation from the communities that I'm bonded with, in the ones that are supposedly here to serve and protect us. A lengthy list of misfortunes continues to fuel animosities and mistrust between the two factions. As time goes on, with the increased usage of media, footage of police brutality, and misuse of the law emerging, it stirred up more anger and various movements were formed.

Growing up in my household, they didn't preach hatred towards law enforcement, just a simple "mind your own business and don't bother having conversations with them to avoid any speculations from people." The most was maybe greeting back and go about your day for the sake of manners, but basically to walk the other way. On the other hand, I also grew up on stories of the corruption of police back home on kidnapping, bribery, etc.

I met some nice cops who would greet with a big smile and even try to joke around. Then there are cops that should honestly take a class on how to stop giving generic reasons like, "Oh, there was a home invasion and they were wearing blah blah (listing out all of the similar clothing and coincidentally the same area) ..." Sometimes, I wished my friends would have different layers of clothing underneath, so they can switch before being pulled over and see if they still "match the description." But no matter what it was, I just felt uneasy when I was walking past officers.

When I am by myself or with my Asian friends, I don't really have any run-ins with the police. They give off a relaxed demeanor and that was the end of it. However, when I am with my black peers, that's when experiences become... unpredictable, from being pulled over to prolonged interrogation and searches. They usually left me alone while going after my companions, except for a few incidents in Durham and Peel, where I was left with a rather bitter aftertaste.

I wanted to touch on a bit of carding; it's not so much the act of carding that bothers me, it's how those in society who are of other minorities would be giving the most support towards carding. I remember I was shocked at other non-black peers in my law class's thoughts about it.

Our teacher had us read an article in the newspaper on bringing back police carding as a way to "tackle the increasing gun violence." Though I may not publicly express my views, I am very much passionately against this ridiculous misuse of power. Though there were one or two black peers, they sat in silence as I went back and forth with other classmates before the teacher, who was agreeing with me, had to move on with the class before it got ugly. "Well, they have to start somewhere" was a line that drove me over the edge. Would they say that if it were their friends, let alone their family members, especially they looked the same in the eyes of the law? Would they continue to say that if it were their people who had been stripped of their dignity over the colour of their skin? I had to write out this more than a decade old rant about carding. What are your thoughts on it?

"A Cop is always a Cop" is a saying that I would always hear from my friends. To become one of them is cut all ties with your inner circle and for them to eliminate any individuality someone once had. Though I am against the ones who are clearly power hungry and trigger happy, racist, etc. and I can write a whole book on corruption within the law enforcement, I always pondered on the fact of "aren't they human too?" Don't they have families, emotions, hobbies and – the one thing I want to emphasize – unresolved baggage they carry? Or the ones who enter the force with genuine good intentions but just like in many other paths in life, certain situations start to mold a person's character.

I remember I had some friends who showed interest in getting enrolled into police school, and they got the typical reaction you would expect in their surroundings: informant, rat, sellout. Not to mention being cut off and receiving other not so nice messages. Even I felt a way when I first heard of their goals; my natural instinct was to deter them from pursuing their dream career for several reasons. I feared for their safety if they were to go back into their neighbourhoods or bump into their old crews, and deep inside I feared that the friendship we once had would dissolve quickly, that I would have to distance myself for the sake of my well-being. I started to fidget my fingers as they shared with me about the process but in the end, they ended up pursuing another career path.

While I felt a blanket of relief covering over me, I couldn't shake off the tiny guilt for not supporting them in their passion. To this day, I feel like they were just settling and a part of me wondered if I played a role in their decision; I tend to be an overthinker. But if they did end up becoming a cop, would I have looked at them differently and put them into the same category as "piglets" and the "po po"? Would I defend that they are more than a label, just like how I defended my other friends who were and are charged and accused as criminals, that I refuse to view them as leftovers or trash? Would I have been able to see the same person I knew a good portion of my life, or another enemy with a badge and a uniform... I may never know.

Though I never had any personal run-ins with correctional officers, I felt the need to touch on this, because I have friends who have different experiences with them. I had friends who were in the street life and ended up taking up positions in the correctional sector because of the pay they offered. Others wanted to make a difference because of their own personal negative and positive experiences with C.O. I wasn't too much of a fan, because I have lost friends due to abuse and negligence of basic human rights, such as medical care, from the officers. Also, for those who know about the corruption, I wonder why they aren't locked up with the inmates for similar things.

But I guess there are always two sides and loopholes to a story, so who am I to really judge? I do, however, have friends who have that one C.O. that took the time to support them to the best of their abilities, so even though it is super scarce, I can still see some humanity and even that glimmer of hope made a big difference.

It took me a long time and lots of back and forth writing this segment. Out of all the pieces I wrote, this particular piece brought the most feeling of uneasiness for me to share with all of my readers. I do understand that I have opened cans of worms and it is my intention to spark discomfort and also deeper thought in my audience. We pray, hope, protest and demand change, yet we have a habit of avoiding the necessary steps to head towards actual change, and yet it has to start from somewhere. Even to be in the same space and have those conversations has been a big hurdle for most and still is, including for me. One of my placements proved that I become stiff and silent around officers, which just shows the passive aggression, but it delivers the same message as others who would be more defensive and speak out. I have allowed a couple of folks to read and give insight and all of them in the end wanted me to expand more on this piece. But I have to be brutally honest, that I have not reached that point where my views are neutral enough for me to feel comfortable enough to write more about the other side. However, I am willing to introduce people who are willing to take the extra step, so contact me and we can get things rolling. I sincerely want to give thanks to several people for all the conversations and pushing me outside my comfort zone when I was writing this piece. To all my readers, I want to thank you for reading all of it with an open heart and please have this dialogue with me if we were to meet or through technology.

Dilemma

They blame the community for being silent
But will they truly protect if we
Started snitching?

Unless you a mob boss or an undercover
Then what the fuck is a witness protection.

Your name stated on the paper
You think they care about repercussions?

Once they raid for that promotion
"You're on your own, rat"
They laugh amongst their peers
Being comfortable within their office.

Hood Chronicles Song List Part - IV

Mad Linqz - Mama
Brizz - Be My Purpose
Pinky - Dem Thugs
Nathan Baya Feat. Al Doex - I Wish
Papoose - Law Library (be sure to listen to Part 1 till Part 8)
Papa Corleone - 14
Trill Fam- Memories
Gemini aka DaGenius - Welcome To DeepRock City
Juice CR - Get a Bag Freestyle
Robin Banks x FB - Raised In
Ludacris Ft. Mary J Blig e- Runaway Love
Hood - It's Up To You
Lady Luck Feat. Jhonnie - No Friend Of Mine
B.G. Feat. Mannie Fresh - My Hood
Bone Thugs-N-Harmony - I've Tried
Geezy Loc - Look Up In The Sky
I-Octane - Lose A Friend
DMX - Where The Hood at
Csin - Barrel Cry
Sizzla - Be Strong
Stack Bundlez - Wife Of Hustlers
Boosie Badazz - My Brother's Keeper
Baby Grhyme Feat. J-Soul - My Mother
Nix The Truth Feat.OTG Gnasty x Luke Melody - It's Like This
Renee Ashanta Henry - Reflections
Heavy Steve - Acoustic Effort
Boosie Badazz - Chasin My Dream
J Jon - Feel Pretty Again
Kaptaiin - Sweet Sorrow
Loco City - Never Know
Webbie Feat. LeToya Luckett - I Miss You

Surauchie - Sometimes
The Dying Thief - H.O.P.E.
EIGHTY - The Real
Point Blank - Born And Raised In The Ghetto
The Dying Thief Feat. Saldo - Be Okay
Star Dat Prince - Success
C-Murder - Ghetto Boy
Sling Dadz Feat. Keon Love - Strive
Trill Fam - Lay Me Down
Stack Bundles - Wives of Hustlers
Dynesti Williams - Guaranteed High
Robin Banks - Slumz
Gangis Khan - Family

family bbq potluck
parties justice faith story
friendship youth community
YGs grandparents ride block
food life police letters prison streetz music
ghetto art jail snitch peace
die mosaic unity
love OGs voices hood
hope parenthood
gun court war
children
lessons violence
death

Freestyle (Bonus)

Till Hoods Rip Us Apart

Together

We didn't know what happened,
Everyone warned us
Not to dig deeper in the trenches.

Our hearts would not listen,
Our thoughts refuse to remain silent.

We allowed ourselves to be consumed in love…
Maybe it was just a deadly infatuation.

Why we allow invisible lines to call the shots?
Turning kids who played in the same playgrounds
Becoming enemies as grown ups.

ACT I

Her

We were born a street apart.
Same schools and same class.

Even with our circumstances
We were both smart.
Excelling in our studies
We both got scholarships to travel abroad.

Our common interest was to come back to the hood.
We both wanted to put food back in the hood.

Though we were from different blocks…

We both had the same passion to tackle the root cause.

But the hoods never wanted to move on.
A beef from the early '60s
Continue to drench blood.

All because we are separated by names the government
    gave us,
We have to suffer for our undying love?

Him

I didn't want to fall for her.
Her neighbours are my homies' murderers.

They rep the south,
I rep the north,
Even though we were best friends back in elementary,
High school is when they wanted to bring talks.

They tortured my boy Rich,
All because he went to their self-proclaimed store
To buy a drink.

"He went into our turf,"
His killer spoke in pride,
No guilt on his face
As both families cried.

He continued to smirk,
Even when he died in his cell block
Just after serving a short time.

She would be everything my crew warned me about.
Bright and beautiful,

A perfect chick for setups.

But her eyes put me into a headspace…
I can't get out.

She is the one for me…
I'm willing to risk it all!

Or….
Do I remain loyal
To my brothers,
The ones that took the charge,
Never allowed me to fall……

ACT II

Scene 1- In an abandoned house

Narrator

A tale that continues to happen in secrecy.
Most know their affairs would end in tragedy.

Forbidden love that would eventually come to light…
Or a love that was one-sided
That would end with a price.

Woe to the lovers
That hoods tear apart.

Paranoid when going out,
So no one would get caught.

Woe to the lovers

Where introducing friends
Is not an option.

Keeping a love away
Even from families,
Because the game
Got everyone tripping.

Her

I can't sleep at night
Without you laying next to my side

Him

We must keep it on the low,
Be careful!
Or our neighbours will know.

Her

How much longer must we creep at night.
I'm starting to feel like a mistress…
Is there something you not telling me?
Do you have a wife?

Him

My love
Don't entertain your mind
With such nonsense.

You're aware of our situation,
Fate has forged a wedge between us.
We cannot attract more attention.

And so,
The lovers continue to see each other during the darkest
    of nights.
Part ways before their intimacy attracted eyes and lips.

But a love so potent cannot walk in the shadows for long,
Because true love radiates like desert sun.

Not long after,
Family and friends start interrogating
From both sides……

ACT III

Scene 1– Her House

Her Brother

My dear sister,
Why are you staying out so late at night?

Her

Just with my friends' brother.
Am I not allowed to have a social life?

Her Brother

Of course!
No doubt!!
When two or more gather

Voices of communities and laughter can be heard heavens
　　around!!!
But sister,
I must ask…
There are hearts from Cupid's arrow
Pierced in your chest.

Tell me who he is,
So our families can wine and dine together
To each other's content.

Her

I do not know what you speak of.

Her Brother

Is it Jerome two doors down?
Tyrone or Shaq?
Ohh
I know
I know,
It's Obinna,
At least he also made it.

silence

Oh dear
Is it Gully from the south?
I didn't know my sister had a taste for bad boys,
We need to sit down!
chuckles

Her

No, brother.
My heart will not be captured by their hands,
Nor will my lips meet theirs.
My love is an offering from The Northern Winds,
In a nearby place of
The Land of Frost Giants.

His love provides warmth and comfort
From such a frozen place.

Her Brother

The Land of Frost?
This thief who stole your heart against your will
Is from the wretched North?!
How could you!
Why would you?!
Turning your back against your own flesh and blood!!
Now we must have a sit down
Before things do go south!!!

Her

Please, brother, relax!
There are no rumours at all!!

Her Brother

How naive are you.
To believe that gossip aren't dandelions becoming
    pappus
To spread among the wild.
You know how powerful a mustard seed is…

Now being assisted with a winter breeze!

Her

Brother
I –

Her Brother

Enough is enough!
I'm calling my boys
To settle the score
RIGHT NOW!!

Scene 2 – His House

His Grandma

What is troubling you my child,
You wear a frown with no shame.
Don't you have a pinch of your pride
Left in your skull?
Tell Granny
Everything!

Him

I love her.

His Grandma

I know…

Don't look so surprised,

You look like you have seen God's kingdom with your
    eyes!
Granny knows best…
I watched you grow,
Taken care of you since your mom passed.
Your father has been in and out of the picture,
So the streets became the dad figure.

I sent my prayers dawn till dusk.
Hoping the Lord would send His angels to take my cries
    up.

And then He answered in the form
That mankind known
But have fully grasped the unknown.

I have watched your exterior shell melt in the name of
    love.

Now, my child,
What is wrong?

Does she not satisfy the quench in your heart?

Him

She is like the rain
That breaks my drought.
I am like the thorns
Protecting her rose.
We both shelter each other
From hail and dust storms.

We are so close
But so apart.

His Grandma

Because you allow places that we don't own
Dictate who you can and who you can't love?

Him

Her people killed Rich.

His Grandma

And it didn't stop you before,
Why now?

Him

They asking me about her.

His Grandma

Then move far away.

Him

What about you Granny?

His Grandma

Who mention I wouldn't come along?
I can't stand this neighbourhood at times.

I watched morals and foundation in all their glory,
Become ruins and now they are crumbled.

We shall all travel to a distant land…

Where stupidity is not the root cause of evil.

Him

Thank you, Granny.

His Grandma

Now go get her,
While I prepare for our departure.

We can stay by my sister until you can pick up your feet,
'Bout time I can go out for an adventure.

Scene III – Her Place

Her

sobbing Brother, let me out,
Why am I a prisoner
Over something that nothing would've stopped?

Her Brother

Once we get rid of that rodent
You'll move on
He'll be a mere memory.
What you think is love
Will be flushed away
Just like his worthless body.

You will thank me later, sister,
Once this pest has been eliminated from our lives,
I do not mind temporary flames from your eyes

Than to be frozen in a tundra for your crimes.

Her

You'll regret this, brother!
True love conquers all!!

Her Brother

What do you know about anything?
You have not fully experienced your youth!

I'll have my men gathered up.
Tonight the snow will melt
As we rejoice in our wine
Quenched from shedding tainted blood!

ACT IV

Scene I – At a nearby park

Him

Where is my love?
I tried calling and texting.
Maybe she is asleep?
I'll give some time
Before I awaken her from her slumber.

Her Brother

I had enough of this
Go back where you come from!
Before you become the living dead

I suggest that you run off!!

Him

I'm not here to quarrel
I only want
What's mine.

Her Brother

My sister
Is
Not
Your
Property!

Him

The love is consensual on both sides.

Her Brother

Don't bring out a wildfire that you cannot tame.

Him

Learn to mind your own business
Before your life is at stake!

Her Brother

Talk to me again you scoundrel!

points a gun

And you won't see the light again!!

Him

Take your best shot!
Your aim won't change a damn thing!!
My tomb will be engraved with her sweetness
My name her voice will sing!!!
Has your heart became so cold
By this blindness
That these hoods got a hold?
The gang will hold you down for so long
Why make something so small into a gang war?

His Brother

You fool dare speak to me
In such tone?
Think you're brave until you meet with your Lord

pulls the trigger

Him

dodges bullet

Just remember we were once friends
Before your father figures dragged us into this endless
    war!

Her Brother

Don't you dare bring up my Masters' names.

Him

Why are you acting like a slave?
Listening to orders
Without questioning
I know you....
I know the loss of your father caused you
Much pain!

Her Brother

Be quiet!

points the gun, ready to shoot

Him

jumps over a bench and runs to some trees to take cover

I don't want to continue
Just leave us alone!
The spell has polluted into your heart....
No truth can seep into that hardened shell...
No more can be done!!
Leave us alone, my in-law I must disown...
I am more than happy to obligate
Not to show my face no more!!!

Scene II – Her place

Her

I will not stand for this
I must get out of here at once!

looks through her drawers and under her bed

I'll plan my escape
I just need to gather up some stuff!!

continues to search

My love
Proceed with caution

My brother is obsessed with his dawgs
And his existence reeks of demons.

The brother we've all known
From childhood,
Was suffocated to death
By his agonizing backstory.

grabs a bobby pin and starts to unlock the door

My love
If fate decides that one must go....
Please make sure he dies in peace,
A quick death you must bestow!

struggles to pick the lock on the door

Enough of this insolence!!!

scurries to her closet and kneels down and runs her fingers on the wood tiles

May my cries to Ekwensu be answered
So I can save my sweet Dearest's life!!!!

Scene III – In the abandoned house

Her Brother

Coward!
Stop intertwining with the goddess of shadows,
The shelters you seek are becoming scarce
For your greed will cause famines.
Come out and face me!

Him

Please stop provoking a monster you cannot defeat.
Blinded rage only feeds The Devil
Unspeakable slaughters that lifeless objects would
tremble at its feet.

The answers are within you.
Why not conquer them?
Instead of harming innocent people.

The war you speak of
Is more on yourself!
I have already put aside my vengeance
To see the good in you

My long-time friend.

Her Brother

Continue to walk amongst the realms of illusion.
Continue to dance among your fantasies that had drained
    any ounce of intelligence.
This myth you speak of
Exists no more....

This person you once called friend
Has lived off the remains of your loved one's riches.

Him

appears from the shadows behind with a knife

Why must you continue to fill up the pastures with the
    living dead?
Why must you continue to challenge?!

His Brother

Let us enter the chambers of torment together!

Narrator

A battle that could cause Atlas to stumble...
Draining oceans into the universe.

Animosity too steep to be recovered...

These two rivals continue to clash until one spills
While the other emerges as the victor.

A blade made from the ice titans
Versus
Fireworks made out of sinister substance.

Struggling to gain control
Now one had upper hand
Waiting to deliver that final blow

Ending just one battle
From a never-ending war.

Her Brother

on top with a gun to the head while catching his breath

Did you really think that you had found favour in the
    gods' eyes to defeat me?!

You should have accepted my offer of mercy
And drag your wretched feet into exile.
But you took this choice...
Now may you not find rest
In unmarked graves
Where you belong

Him

May fallen soldiers
Return this deed
To generations after you fall....

Her Brother

SILENCE!

finger pressing on the trigger but suddenly looks up

How could you betray....

clutches chest

I will forever curse you for this, my dear sis...

collapses onto the concrete

Narrator

Death ripped across allied nations
Ending a bond that lasted since birth.

How could the same one that you walked alongside
Broke bread with and rested in the same palace...
Be the one to send you back
Into the spiritual world.

Him

gets up and stares at the lifeless body

My love
How could you....

looks at her in shock

Her

He would've killed you
If I got here any later!

Him

stares at her hand

He was your own kin...

Her

I refuse to witness...

My Dearest...

What is the meaning of this!

slowly backs away

Why is there a stone golem
Taking over my kind giant?!

<u>Him</u>

We end this cycle now...

walks slowly towards her with a bloody knife and gun

To Be Continued...

ABOUT THE AUTHOR

Born in the early '90s, Gloria Sze-Ming O'koye (G.L. Glowz) was raised in Toronto, Ontario. Influenced since birth by her musically talented mother who had previously been a piano teacher and choir director, Gloria realized her passion for music and love for creative writing.

As Gloria got older, she discovered how hectic and discouraging life can be. With the onset of 2012, she dedicated herself to be a Voice for the Voiceless. A talented songwriter for 13 years and a dedicated short story writer for the past 18 years, her involvement in the poetry scene started with the performance of her most popular poem "Letter to My Angel" at Fallen Soldiers in 2013.

Gloria incorporates choruses and hooks as techniques in her poetry. She considers her grandmother and her daughters to be her motivation for writing. Her biggest influences include cultural reggae and '90s rap, and artists T-Rell, Jah Vinci, Tupac, Plies, Nas, Lil' Boosie, Heartless G, DMX, and Blacus Ninjah.

Moving around the city frequently and getting exposed to various lifestyles, Gloria's writing reflects on her personal experience and the lives of people surrounding her. She is passionate about building relationships with different communities and has been an active member in community engagements across the GTA since 2010.

Gloria recently self-published her debut book, *A Kintsugi Memoir*, in October 2018, a collection of short stories and reflections.

www.ingramcontent.com/pod-product-compliance
Lightning Source LLC
Chambersburg PA
CBHW070452030726
47503CB00004B/1010